MATTHEW WOLF

VISIONS OF A HIDDEN

A RONIN SAGA SHORT STORY

VISIONS OF A HIDDEN
A Ronin Saga Short Story
Matthew Wolf

Learn more at www.matt-wolf.com

MATTHEW WOLF

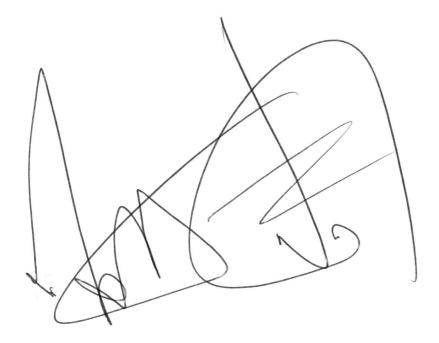

VISIONS OF A HIDDEN

A RONIN SAGA SHORT STORY

CONTENTS

THE THREE ELF BOYS sat silently, nervously. They were uncertain why they had been chosen, only certain that they had. They were young, especially for elves, each younger than their sixth spring. The eldest of these three was a long brown-haired boy with hard eyes named Rydel. He knew that the tall elf before them was someone to be feared.

On the big elf's back was a grand-looking cloak that brushed the floor. As Rydel looked at the cloak, his eyes strangely hurt. The big elf shifted subtly and as he did the cloak shimmered, *blending* with its surroundings as he moved. Rydel was in awe, but the cloak paled compared to the object dangling at the big elf's hip.

A sword like out of the stories...

The big elf stood with one hand on a green-handled blade at his waist, as he talked with an elf with a white beard. Much older, this one wore fancy white robes with green embroidered vines and leaves. Rydel had seen clothes like that before when his mother had pointed to the king and queen as they'd strode through the dappled lit forest.

The two elves were whispering now, but their words were loud enough to be heard by Rydel's keen ears. Perhaps they didn't know or didn't care, but he listened as the hardened, younger-looking one asked, "King Gias wishes this? You're certain?" The elf wasn't just tall. He was big. Rydel had seen strong elves like the Terma, but this man's simple green clothing didn't hide his bulging arms and thick neck. He must've been the biggest elf Rydel had ever seen. Middling in years for an elf, perhaps Rydel's father's age, but the tough look on his face made him look much older still. Rydel had never seen anyone look so mean. He towered over them and cast occasional unsettling glances at the three boys who sat on their knees in the green glade, trembling. On Rydel's right, the little black-haired boy sniffled, as if holding back tears; while the blonde-haired boy to his left held a distant wide-eyed gaze as if he was imagining being someplace very far from here.

"From his mouth to my ears," said the old elf dutifully. "It is the King's own wish."

The big elf growled in frustration. "Why now? Why bring back the old ways now? We are at peace. Fractured and divided from the other Great Kingdoms, but at peace. What is he preparing for?"

The old elf shook his head, fine, straight white beard swaying. "I can't say, but King Gias is not one to frighten easily. You know this above all others, Trinaden." *Trinaden... was that the big elf's name?*

King Gias. Rydel knew that name too. Lord of all the elves and ruler of the Great Kingdom of Leaf. *King Gias ordered this?* Rydel's mother hadn't been able to tell him anything. She had just said she loved him very much, to trust that, and listen to the old elf. That was yesterday. Shortly after, the old one had come and collected him, tears in his mother's eyes as she had watched him leave. They had walked in silence for what felt like ages until they reached the green glade and the mean-looking master Trinaden. The other two boys had been waiting when he had arrived.

"You know more than you're saying, Lorsan," growled the mean-looking elf.

The old elf, Lorsan, sighed. "If I had to guess, the King sees something on the horizon we cannot. These boys will be needed one day. Either way, they are yours now," Lorsan said gravely, nodding his head to Rydel and the other two at his side. "Their provisions will be cared for. Their training and all else is yours to oversee."

Trinaden grunted at last. "So be it. I will do what I can. But when I'm done with them, they won't be boys. They might not even be elves."

The way he said it frightened Rydel. *Might... not even be elves? What did he mean?*

Trinaden had a haunted look on his face, then it passed and only a hard craggy exterior remained.When Lorsan left, the tall elf turned to them, silent for a long moment. Rydel watched the sword with keen interest. He couldn't stop staring at it. It had a strange emerald handle and a green glow emanated from within the sheath. Then Rydel spotted the elf's gnarled hands. They had thick calluses and many tiny white scars. The big elf spoke in a voice like thunder and gravel. "My name is Trinaden dal' Melowyn, but you will call me Master."

The two boys at Rydel's side gave slow nods.

Trinaden unsheathed his blade in a rush, pointing to them. His expression was cold and calculated, lacking hatred or remorse. "Words have power. I would have you say it now."

"Master," the two boys echoed in trembling voices.

Rydel felt their fear, saw their wide terrified eyes in the corner of his vision. He knew he should be scared, too. He knew that this elf was death— that this blade was something the likes he'd never seen before. Not from the Mela, not even the Terma, supposedly the strongest of all Elvin warriors and guards, to the King himself. Trinaden was different still. Instead, Rydel could only stare at the blade before him. The weapon hovered before his eyes, a glistening point of steel with a green hue, drawing him in.

"You like the blade, boy?" Trina—*Master* asked.

Rydel could only nod.

"You've got a fine eye for steel, if that is even its origins, though I doubt it very much. It's a leafblade, an ancient relic belonging to warriors from a time long before you were born." Rydel didn't know what that meant, but it sounded special. "Your name, what is it?"

"Ry-rydel," Rydel stuttered. Without warning, the blade sliced and a small bloody pain stung Rydel on the cheek. Fingers unconsciously reached up and felt the split skin and pooling warm blood. Anger and fear flashed inside him. Trinaden's expression hadn't altered a single hair. It remained cold, mean, uncaring, and... expectant. Rydel realized his mistake. "*Master*," Rydel added quickly.

Master Trinaden inclined his head, slightly, and sheathed the leafblade. "Understand this," the big elf announced. "Your parents gave you up. Your brothers, sisters, friends—you have none. I am your family, and I am not your family. You are mine now to do as I will, to craft and mold to one purpose. To wield this," he lifted the green-hued sword, "and become a leafbearer. Once you have passed your training, you will bear the leafblade, and become something more, something none have seen in a thousand years."

"Leafbearer... Master?" The little boy to Rydel's left asked in a shaky voice. He was the blonde-haired elf and the youngest of the three. His long pointed ears poked out from his hair. He had inquisitive emerald eyes and a small, nervous smile. "What are Leafbearers?"

"Royal warriors to the Ronin themselves, though some called them the Hidden. The most powerful and revered warriors in all Farhaven. You will become that weapon. If you do not listen as I say, you will be cast out. It will not be easy. You will hurt. You will make pain your friend. I will not lie to you. Even if you do as I say, you may die," he said and let it sink in. Rydel realized his body was shivering of its own accord. "But," the big elf said with a slim smile—the first and last it looked like he'd ever make, "you will be something the likes of which the world has not seen for many an age."

"What must we do?" Rydel asked. The others looked to him, surprised. His mother had said to trust that old elf, Lorsan, and Lorsan had put his faith in Trinaden. Rydel would do whatever it took to see his mother again.

"So eager already, young elf?" Master Trinaden asked, then obliged his head. "The task is simple, but far from easy: withstand my tutelage, speak the oaths, and finally survive the Trial of the Forest. Then, and only then, will you receive your blades and have the honor of being called a Hidden, a Leafbearer."

Rydel swallowed and heard the others do the same.

"Now, names," Master Trinaden ordered and pointed to the small towheaded boy at Rydel's side.

"Hadrian," the blonde boy answered timidly.

The long raven-haired boy and the middle in age replied, "Dryan." He had little scrolls like curling vines under his bright blue eyes, a rare but not unheard of birthmark for elves. His voice too had a keener, higher edge to it, and his face looked like one made for mischief—more sharply angled eyes that flitted about nervously.

Master grunted. "Good."

Master then showed them to their rooms. They were cramped quarters with three beds huddled against the far wall. There was nothing else. No decorations aside from a single window that peered into the verdant, glowing green woods of Eldas, the city of leaf. "This is where you will stay," Master Trinaden announced. "My room is off-limits. We eat in the living room, and training starts anywhere I say it does."

All three stared at the tiny cots, and Master Trinaden answered their unasked question, "You will learn to live sparsely. You are hidden-in-training, not boys, and you'll have no need of toys or material possessions. Your bodies, your very souls now belong to a higher calling—in light of this, worldly items are meaningless." He let the words sink in, then announced, "In the morning we begin. Be ready." Without another word, he shut the door with a bang making the three boys jump.

Unsure of what else to do, Rydel began to silently unpack his meager belongings. The others did the same when the boy with black hair began to cry. His sobs and little sniffles continued as he half-heartedly laid his clothes in a stack beside his small cot.

Rydel didn't know what to say. He wanted comfort himself, so he just stood frozen. Hadrian left his bedside and put his arm around Dryan's shoulders. Rydel watched them. Tears stained their faces and they wore fearful expressions. "Do you think he's... do you think it's true?" Hadrian asked Rydel. "Our family, our friends... they're gone?"

Rydel could only nod.

"Why? Why us?" Hadrian asked.

"I wanna go home," the little boy with black-hair said in a sniffly whine.

Rydel turned away. Anger, fear, and uncertainty swirled inside him when he felt something in his pack—it was the small stone his mother had given him. They weren't allowed to bring anything aside from clothes, but he'd hidden it. Now he tucked it under his pillow and turned back to the other two. *They're afraid, and so am I, but... My mother said to be brave.* As the oldest, this was his duty. It sounded like something his father would say.

His father had barely spoken to him, but when he had, he'd demanded Rydel to be strong, to overcome his fear. His mother had demanded him to care. Rydel envisioned his mother's face and drew a deep breath, summoning his courage. He placed his hands on their shoulders. The two boys looked up at him with big, watery eyes, and he smiled as wide as he could, though he was certain they could see how scared he was, too. Mustering his voice, Rydel declared, "He was wrong. This is our home. We are brothers now, and we will protect each other. I won't let anything happen to you two." Hadrian smiled, and Dryan nodded. "I promise." And he meant it.

Having been exhausted, they curled up in their hard cots and found slumber. When Rydel awoke later in the night to the creaking of floorboards, he found the other two were in his bed. In the morning, Master Trinaden had found them, huddled and bleary-eyed, but he hadn't said a word. Somehow, Rydel knew it had been a onetime thing.

In the morning, as promised, they trained. The days were long. They ate little and drank less. Sleep was scarce. Chores filled any gaps not dedicated to some form of training. Climbing on rocks, pushing heavy logs, swimming upriver, and a thousand other exercises became rote. Master trained them to the bone. Crying or complaining was quickly ruled out as it only made Master work them harder. Less work meant less food, and less food meant they were too tired to work. So the more they worked, the more they ate. Some days their bodies wouldn't move. Rydel would struggle to lift an arm or a leg, the fatigued muscles feeling like glass shards embedded into his leaden limbs.

On these days, when they were too exhausted to move—and Trinaden could tell when they were faking it—Rydel was allowed to pick a book from Master's shelf, and they would read.

Master Trinaden followed his own advice of an austere life, and the hut wasn't much to look at. There were only four rooms in the hut. Their cramped quarters, Master's, which was forbidden to enter at all times, a spare room, and the living room. The living room could be described as minimalistic, its decorations as sparse as a freshly picked bone. It held only a metal stove, a few cabinets for essentials, and a fireplace that remained cold unless it was winter. Here, above the mantle, the leafblade hung when not on Master's waist. Three chairs and a table sat in the center. Among these bare necessities, it bore one peculiarity.

Books.

They lined every wall. Even the spare bedroom was devoted entirely to the housing of all varieties of tomes, codex, parchments, and journals.

The hut held books on all subjects: philosophy, history, languages, geography, government, economics, herb lore, medicine, and any subject Rydel could imagine or wish to learn.

Once when Rydel was only a few summers old, he remembered his mother taking him to a library in Eldas. It had been much bigger and fancier, with white columns. Several stories tall, it was filled with scholars and all sorts of important folk. Humble as Master Trinaden's house was, his collection was impressive. Most of the books were old and seemed special. After a time it seemed Trinaden's goal was for Rydel and the others to read them all. Master Trinaden being Master Trinanden made everything into a test. When they would fail to remember a passage or an important fact, they would be forced to sleep outside in the cold or do some menial task like peel a hundred potatoes with their fingernails. Rydel quickly noticed that Master Trinaden never yelled or raged at them. He had no need. He would simply look at them with his frozen blue eyes until they jumped to task. Despite this, Rydel enjoyed reading days. When he'd asked timidly why warriors needed to read, Trinaden's answer was simple: *An ignorant warrior is a dead warrior. You must keep your mind as sharp as your blade. For both are weapons no warrior can do without. You will learn these texts as well as you know your blade to come, if not better.*

He'd laughed and told Master it was impossible to read that many books.

Trinaden had pulled a tome off the shelf and asked Rydel to flip to a random page. Upon doing so, Trinaden spoke, reciting the *Herbology of the Aster Plains* word for word. Stunned, Rydel felt a renewed fear of this elf whom he had assumed was more brawn than brain, and he thought he understood Trinaden's words a little better.

It wasn't long before Master had them train with weapons.

Rydel learned the bow first. *To kill from afar is a more powerful tool than even the sharpest sword,* said Master.

Then he learned the staff: a long staff, then a quarterstaff, and finally all the way down to a broken broom handle. They laughed when Master had shown it at first. When Master used it to bruise them from head to toe with his eyes closed, all laughing ceased. Of course, different weights and sizes required slightly different moves. They would spend days practicing the perfect strike, block, parry or redirect. Only once they'd mastered the basics to Trinaden's very particular satisfaction did they progress. And Master Trinaden was very particular. Moreover, their advancement was together, or not at all. Another time, Rydel and Dryan had stayed up all night with Hadrian teaching him the correct movements for the quarterstaff.

After basics, they'd learn complex forms to put the moves into patterns to make them become innate. *Instinctual,* Trinaden had said. *You will live and breathe these moves. You will do them in your sleep.* He was right. Rydel woke at night more than once performing complex strikes and blocks. Other times while doing chores, like pouring water, he found his feet moving in subtle, but intricate patterns of footwork until he'd realized what he was doing. After the forms came the practice dummies.

The dummies were wooden poles with arms. They were set up in the hut's enclosed glade. On these, they'd learn the proper vital targets and to hit as hard as they could. Striking with fists or legs, the wooden dummy toughened their limbs. When questioning why they trained so much without weapons, Trinaden had told them: *you are the weapon. A sword or staff is merely a tool.* At first, while striking the wooden dummy, Rydel felt his skin split and bruise. He'd go to bed so hurt that sleeping was near impossible. But over days, his skin, his muscle, his very bone hardened. It didn't take long until he could hit the wooden dummy as hard as he could with only minimal pain.

They also learned when to use weapons. Some were for close quarters, others for distance. They learned to disarm, and how to incorporate strikes, kicks, joint locks, and pressure points. *A single strike to the right place is worth a hundred others to the wrong ones.* They began to get used to their master repeating these phrases, his grating voice a chorus to their pain. The words were drilled into their heads until Trinaden's expressions became truth. Only once they'd shown complete mastery of every element, did they move to the true test and the application of their skills: sparring.

This was Rydel's favorite part.

Rydel loved sparring Dryan and Hadrian, and the others took a liking to it as well. It was a test among brothers and a showcase of their endless hours of hard work. Rydel quickly learned their different skill sets.

Hadrian, though younger than Rydel, was taller, broader, and undoubtedly the strongest. He was stronger than both Rydel and Dryan by a good bit. By the age of seven, he could even hoist a log over his head that required Dryan and Rydel together. Dryan was the fastest and most agile. Nimbly he'd duck and dodge Hadrian and Rydel's blows and return swift strikes of his own. Rydel was a combination of the two. Neither was he as strong as Hadrian or as quick as Dryan, but he held the balance of both, and for that, the two respected him greatly and acknowledged him as their leader of sorts.

They learned how to wield a vast array of weapons from behemoth hammers, heavy-headed great axes, or far-reaching polearms, to small agile weapons like claws, swordbreakers, knives, and a hundred other tools of warfare. He had never known so many types of weapons had existed. All the while, Rydel's annoyance grew along with a strange burning desire founded on that first day: no swords like the leafblade. He hadn't touched a real sword yet, only wooden imitations. Instead, when they were tired and beaten like a sack of bruised potatoes, he would fall into a heap on the floor, unable to even reach his room. Lying, beaten and bone-tired, he would stare up at the leafblade where it hung above the mantel. Daily he'd watch it longingly as it swayed at Master's hip or hung about their small hut like a fruit just out of reach. *It will be mine one day,* he would vow again and again, until this, too, became Rydel's creed.

As time passed, they grew bigger and stronger. With age, their features slowly changed too. Their plump boyish features changed under Master's tutelage. They weren't quite hardened and chiseled, but the fat on Hadrian and Dryan's cheeks hollowed out, the angles coming in more sharply.

Dryan had never lost that perpetual gleam of mischief in his gaze. The vines under his blue eyes had darkened along with his skin, and he appeared almost tan for an elf.

Hadrian grew taller and wider. A smile always donned his face. His jaw was sharp and angular and he seemed excited each time he discovered a new wiry hair on his body. He was quick to measure everything with Rydel, though Dryan's competitive drive was never far behind. Arm-wrestling, feats of jumping, agility contests, spitting contests, and literally anything else could be turned on its head in moment's notice to a sudden challenge. Once they competed to see who had the strongest toes, and another time who could sprint the longest blindfolded without running into something. Rydel had won by not participating in that one. Still, normally Rydel always joined in, if reluctantly. As time went on, he was distantly aware that their once scrawny legs and arms filled out with hardened, compact muscle. Despite the moments of levity and brotherhood carved out of brief necessity, the training was brutal and most days felt more like torture.

Bedtime was plagued with restless sleep. They had to learn to sleep lightly, to wake at a moment's notice. If they snored Master would sneak into their room and beat them. Sleep became a mix of bliss and torment. Their hardships increased evermore as time progressed. They washed with only frozen water that stung like icy splinters. Over time, they grew accustomed to the freezing bite. Rydel was amazed at what one could acclimate to with time.

Master Trinaden, Rydel realized quickly, was an ever-creative genius for their trials.

They learned to run long and hard. Rydel's legs wobbled as they'd run up and down hills, forced to sprint. Once frail and slow, they grew stronger until they loped like wolves, racing lightning-fast wild cormacs through the dense glades. When the time came that miles flew beneath their feet in a blur, Rydel felt an impending fear that a new obstacle was fast approaching. Sure enough, Trinaden forced them to strap rock-filled heavy packs to their bodies. As a final test of their speed, they were required to bring the same colored rocks to their master from one end of Relnas Forest to the other. The journey was a two day's ride on a swift mount and they were to match that time. It was an impossible feat, but so were all Master Trinaden's ordeals.

When the day came, they stood in the dark glade, packs strapped. "Well, shall we?"

After the first few hours, their breaths were all labored. The weight hurt Rydel's ankles with each pounding step, but he saw Dryan was lagging. Rydel neared his smaller brother. The sly-looking elf had sweat straining down his face, pain etching his features. Rydel took off Dryan's pack. His raven-haired brother watched him with his bright, curious blue eyes as Rydel took out stones from Dryan's pack.

"You can't," Dryan said. "We need them all."

Rydel gave a smirk. "We need them all, but he didn't say we had to carry the same amount." And he placed two heavy rocks into his own bag, dreading the pounding pain his ankles were about to endure, but he hid it with a wider grin.

Hadrian neared and took three big stones—one from Rydel's back and two from Dryan's. When Rydel looked to argue, Hadrian lifted a brow. "Come now, brother. You don't want all the fun, do you?"

Miles continued until Rydel's feet felt swollen to the size of dalwat fruits. The dull, repetitive ache in his ankles spread to his knees and he felt them swell as well. Still, they ran, sprinting like the wind. Rydel felt his bones crack—fractures forming in his legs as he ran. He wanted to stop, to lie down or cry out. But in his peripheries, his brothers ran as well, their breaths a chorus in his ears to keep going. Finally, exhausted, his bones aching, his body bleeding... they reached it. In one day they had run the course of Relnas Forest; a journey that would have taken an average human or even an elf a week's trek.

Master Trinaden was waiting for them in a small glade. His shimmering hando cloak, the cloak of the Hidden, blended with the woods behind him as he stood like a statue. A stony expression graced his face, which still looked mean to Rydel to this day. Trinaden could scowl without scowling or stare down a full grown drekkar, a demon of Drymaus forest. His ever-present leafblade was at his side. Rydel emptied their sacks letting rocks spill to the mossy floor, showing them all. Before they had arrived, the burden had been split evenly between only him and Hadrian. Still, they had all made it—broken and battered, they had done it. Trinaden made no move. Finally, he gave a slight nod of approval. That was it. Nevertheless, Rydel felt a wave of warmth at the rare slight praise; though, for a flickering moment, his gaze was mysterious as he looked at Dryan.

The tortures grew more severe.

To increase their pain tolerance, they ran through briar patches or slept in the freezing cold in the dead of winter with only a thin blanket. Yet for every strike they would take, for every run, for every exercise, Master did it with them, harder and faster. This above all else made Rydel not loathe the elf, and like a seedling, his respect grew.

All the while, he trained them to be warriors above warriors.

He trained them not to fear death.

He trained them to be weapons.

Time passed in a strange blur, slow yet fast. Days became months, months became years. If he could have, Rydel would have thought about his past life, about his parents. Instead, the training was the only thing filling his thoughts. Every second was grueling. He needed every morsel of energy and concentration to survive. The pain, exhaustion, and intensity kept him ever-present. If he let his concentration slip, he would fail. And failure wasn't an option. He fell sometimes, though when he did, the others would be there. Hadrian offering a hand, Dryan a nod. Other times, he would be there for them. They were three pillars leaning on one another. As the days went on, the feeling of hardship turned to true pain. More than once Rydel felt the icy grip of darkness slip over his mind, and he thought the embrace of death would take him, free him from the endless torture. Still, every time in that final moment, he pulled himself free or found a glimmer of light. Bruises. Cuts. Broken bones. These all became commonplace until they grew quicker and faster. Their injuries became less and less, though they kept their scars.

One day on the haystacks, Dryan's arrow had missed the center of the target. Trinaden's punishment was for him to sleep outside in the forest in the freezing cold. It was a night so bitter that even the water in their hut had frozen over. He and Hadrian were restricted from doing anything, but as the storm grew worse, Rydel's worry increased until he couldn't help himself. His brother was out there and he wouldn't abandon him to the horrid storm. Hadrian didn't take much convincing. They left and found Dryan covered in a blanket of snow. His normally tan skin was now grey as a pale moon. He was still as death and a black rot had settled on his ears. Rydel knew the signs that Dryan's flesh was dying.

Putting his ear to the smaller elf's chest, he listened for a heartbeat. A faint thump answered. Then another. Soft and staggered.

"Is he…" Hadrian had asked.

"Not yet," Rydel replied. "But he will be if we don't do something about it. Help me get him up."

Hadrian hesitated.

Rydel knew what his friend was thinking. Trinaden would have their heads. There was no defying their master. Years ago it had happened. Dryan had tested their master and the big elf had hung him over a waterfall. The look in Trinaden's eyes was clear back then. He'd have dropped Dryan to his death if the boy had uttered another disobedient word. Now they would have to face Trinaden's same impassive, icy justice if they brought home their friend, even if he was dying. "We can't leave him here, Hadrian," Rydel declared.

Hadrian hesitated.

"We can't let him die," Rydel said more firmly. "He wouldn't leave us." Though he wasn't certain about that. Dryan had always seemed different from them; though he was still their brother. They were all they had, and Rydel had made a promise long ago. *I will protect you.*

"Trinaden will kill us," Hadrian said flatly.

Rydel looked at him. "Then we'll die together."

Hadrian gave a slow smile, then bent and helped him hoist Dryan. They'd hurried home seeing the small hut in the distance—a trail of smoke curled from the riverstone chimney, its roof laden with thick snow, an oddly tranquil sight in light of their dying brother. As the cold picked up, the storm bit deeper—stinging his eyes and face. Long ago his extremities had gone numb along with his face. Through squinted vision, Rydel held onto that image of the warm glow from the windows. Each step like lead, Rydel found the last bit of his energy: in an exhausted voice that hitched from the bitter cold, he rallied Hadrian, "Quickly, bro-brother. We-we're almost there." Frozen as icicles themselves, they reached the door just as Trinaden opened it.

"Le-let us in," Rydel demanded. "He's near frozen. H-he needs a healer and a fire or he'll die."

Master Trinaden didn't move. He stood coolly, his wide shoulders brushing the doorframe. His long fall of blond hair fell into his eyes as he stared down at Rydel. Rydel had grown over the years, but Trinaden still towered over him. His heart thumped, feeling the weight of the elf's stare. "You disobeyed my orders."

16

"He would die," Rydel said, teeth still chattering. "And he still might if you don't get out of our way."

Still, Trinaden remained motionless, blocking their path.

Rydel grit his teeth, his anger festered, taking control. He felt his body shake with rage, overpowering his cold body. "Why? Why train us, why do all this work if you're just going to let us die!"

Master Trinaden smacked Rydel across the face, hard enough that blood splayed from his mouth and he felt a tooth loosen. The blow had been too fast to see. Hadrian and the frozen Dryan collapsed. Sluggish from the cold, Hadrian tried to rush to Rydel's side but a metallic ring cut him short. Master Trinaden pointed his blade to Hadrian's throat, then turned it to Rydel. "You don't understand yet, do you?"

Rydel tasted blood as he stared daggers at his master.

"You will kill, and you will face conditions far worse than this," he said, pointing to the snowstorm. "I'm training you to withstand. One day, not long from now, you will be forced to walk into Drymaus Forest. When that day comes, every ounce of strength and hardship you have garnered will be needed. If Dryan is weak, he will die. That is the way of life and the Hidden's first code. But he's not your responsibility. If you coddle him, he will only show weakness later and get you or others killed then." Rydel looked at Master Trinaden. For the first time in his life, he felt true hatred for the man. He didn't understand him. Trinaden waved a hand of dismissal and stalked inside, but left the door open.

Later that night after the healer had left, Rydel came to Trinaden who sat in his chair staring into the fire. "How is he?" Master Trinaden asked, gazing into the snapping flames.

"He's alive," Rydel said, and couldn't help but add, "barely. The healer said if he'd been out another minute, he'd be dead."

Without asking permission, Rydel turned to leave when—

"Rydel," Trinaden spoke. Then he was silent for a long time, staring at the petulant flames until finally, "Your lives are no longer your lives. If you survive this, you'll be able to change the course of history. Dryan needs to

17

know that this isn't about you. It isn't about me. If you survive, you may very likely save us all."

"What if I don't want to save anyone, what if I just want to go back?" Rydel asked and looked away. "What if I want this all to end and to live a normal life?"

Master Trinaden smiled and finally looked at him. He thought the elf would be mad but instead, he replied, "You will never be normal, Rydel. Even if I or you wished it, you will always be different. You have what I fear Dryan will never have."

"What's that supposed to mean?"

Master Trinaden shook his head. "Dryan... Something eats at the boy's soul that I cannot shave away."

"If he has any darkness," Rydel replied. "It will be your fault. You made him that way tonight."

Trinaden shook his head, "No, boy. No one can make someone evil. Everything is a choice in this world, but some darkness can be born within. Dryan is strong, weaker than you as he stands, but he has the potential to be the strongest of all, though not where it counts."

Dryan, the strongest of all? Was it true? But he asked, "What do you mean where it counts?"

Trinaden's next words were a mere whisper, "The third and final code." And his eyes blazed with the fire's light, "To be a Hidden, above all else means to sacrifice yourself, but never your soul for the greater good. What you did today proved that. You saved your brother despite the pain you knew it would cause you. But you can't lose your soul just to save the world, or the world isn't worth saving." Then something happened that Rydel couldn't quite comprehend. In the flickering firelight, he saw a glistening drop on Trinaden's face. A tear? Trinaden was weeping?

The image stuck with him, even as Rydel went to bed that night. But the next day—training resumed as normal. Dryan recovered slowly, and as he did, something seemed left behind. He lost part of his ear from the black rot of cold but had gained a strange dark gleam in his eyes. When he looked to Master Trinaden, Rydel saw a low terrible rage in his brother's gaze, darker than ever before. It was as if the rot eating at his flesh that night, now ate at his soul. Still, Rydel wasn't sure Trinaden was right. He could hardly blame Dryan. At night, when they had all gone to bed and Dryan thought no one else could hear, Rydel could hear Dryan's low, spiteful curses. His life had almost been taken for nothing more than a missed arrow. Still, Master Trinaden's words had left their mark as well—they lingered in his mind, even louder. *What did he mean, 'we're going to save the world'?* And what was all that about sacrifice?

One morning, Master had left on an errand and in his absence, a rumor grew. The three sat at the table, hunched over their breakfast of gruel. It was a sticky mass of nutrients ground into a glue-like paste, something that would stick to their stomachs and give them energy for the day's training.

Usually, they talked little, but over the days and years, they had formed a bond of mutual respect. They had fought and nearly died. Now, with Master gone for the day in Eldas, they were giddy with the absence of his watchful eyes. They chatted in low tones in the green wood hut, "Do you think... do you think it's today?" Dryan asked. "Swords, real swords! I saw them in the glade. *Metal* blades." For all their hard work, for all they'd learned—they had still yet to train with a sword that wasn't wooden. Rydel's heart, his whole essence, yearned to touch the leafblade that hung above the mantle. The metal blades they had seen as well would be a poor but willing substitute until that day. Rydel kept his thoughts to himself, however, as he was half-heartedly reading from a book while the other two gossiped.

"Today is different. Today we will to train with the Terma," Hadrian announced with a gleam in his eyes.

"You're lying," Dryan said.

"Am not—it's the truth," Hadrian said firmly.

Rydel put his book down, unable to concentrate and eyed Hadrian. "What makes you say that? What do you know that we don't oh-wise-one?"

Hadrian slurped the ground root-based gruel from a bowl and gestured with his wooden spoon, wearing a mischievous smirk, "Because I heard it. From him."

"Master said so?" Dryan asked dubiously.

"From the elf's own mouth. Told the Healers that came yesterday."

"Why?" Rydel asked. "How did you hear this?"

Hadrian shrugged innocently. "Was reading a book behind the woodpile. Master didn't know I was there."

"Why tell the healer?" Rydel asked.

"Don't know," Hadrian said with a shrug. "You're the clever one. But... if I had to make an educated guess," Hadrian smirked his usual wild grin. "I think the healers will be needed if you catch my drift."

"We're going to fight the Terma?" Dryan asked breathlessly.

Rydel felt a surge of excitement. Terma. They were the most powerful and elite of elven warriors, aside from the mysterious, clandestine rank of the Hidden. He tampered down his nervous energy and corrected Dryan, "Spar, Dryan. Not fight. The Terma are elves like us. We don't fight our kind."

Dryan laughed coldly. "We don't fight anything except wooden dummies and haystacks. Truly the most intimidating of opponents."

"Frankly, I'm glad," Hadrian said. "You are both of the same intelligence. I wouldn't trust you with a smarter opponent."

"At least I'm quick enough to dodge their attacks. If Master gave us money, I'd put all my wager on the wooden dummy over you."

"Safe bet," Hadrian admitted.

Dryan smirked in victory, the vines under his eyes crinkling.

"Unless..." Hadrian posed, "by wooden dummy, you're referring to yourself. Then I'd definitely win."

Suddenly, faster than Rydel's eyes could catch, a glob of gooey gruel shot through the air and hit Hadrian in the eye. Hadrian growled, wiping it from his face and swiped a big arm towards Dryan who nimbly, and easily dodged the attack and countered with a flying spoon. This Hadrian caught and rose from his chair with an eager grin and a battle-stance, dual-wielding his spoons as if they were the legendary blades Masamunde and Morrowil, Ronin's blades. Dryan leaped from his chair onto the table with practiced ease and grabbed the wooden bowl, ready to defend himself, dropping into another low expert fighting stance.

Hadrian rolled his heavy shoulders. "I was going to save my energy for the Terma, but I suppose I can warm up on you."

Dryan snorted. "I'll show the Terma what we really can do. Like the gruel, you can have my scraps if there's anything left."

With gruel on Hadrian's face and the deadly serious expression on Dryan's while wielding a wooden bowl that dripped porridge, they both looked ridiculous. Rydel couldn't help smiling when he heard a barely audible creak at the hut's entrance.

"*Master*," Rydel warned. He was too slow as the door banged open.

Master Trinaden stood in the doorway, looming as ever. A bundle dangled in one hand, with his other hand resting on the glowing green blade as usual. Those frozen eyes took in the scene quickly. Rydel sat at the table, book in hand. Hadrian and Dryan stood posed in battle stances like statues until Dryan dropped his shield and the wooden bowl clattered to the table, splattering porridge onto Master Trinaden's black jacket. Dryan flushed red with fear. Hadrian snuck the spoons behind his back. "Master," they all said in unison, bowing their heads.

Rydel waited for the elf to cast his judgment and send them running or some other arduous task. Instead, Master Trinaden ignored the porridge on his jacket. He cast a raised brow at the scene, then tossed the bundle on the table. "Wear these."

Grabbing the jute sack, Rydel extracted three cloth strips. Masks, he realized. Rydel passed one to Dryan and another to Hadrian. "Does this mean, are we... Hidden?" Dryan asked with a hungry gleam in his eyes.

"Not yet," Master Trinidan said. "You are only true Hidden once you get the sword and the cloak that I bestow upon you, and not a moment before that. Right now, you are hidden-in-training, my pupils, and nothing more."

"Then why the masks?" Hadrian asked. "I'm all for fashion accessories, but is this really necessary?"

Trinaden grunted. "It is. Your identities must not be known. From today on, you will wear these at all times. Even amongst each other."

"From what are we hiding?" Rydel asked. "What do we have to fear?"

"To be a Hidden means to be a knife in the dark, nameless and quiet, nothing more, nothing less. You must be an enigma. An impossibility— nonmortal in the eyes of your enemies, and a shadow in the eyes of your allies. Only working behind the scenes can you hope to accomplish the grand tasks that will change the world.

"Furthermore, today we will head to Eldas proper, the Great Kingdom. Today you will put your skills to the test. The masks will hide your identity."

"We're going to Eldas?" Rydel asked. *Eldas. Mother.* Hope and a confluence of emotions he'd pushed down for years now surged forth. He would see his mother.

Master Trinaden nodded.

"Then it's true, we're going to fight the Terma, Master?" Dryan asked eagerly, leaping lightly from the table.

"To *train*," Master corrected.

"Master, why must we hide among our own people? I don't like it," Rydel said, realizing he was shaking with irritation.

"Especially from your own people." Master Trinaden fixed him with a level stare.

"But, they are our people. We fight for them. There are no enemies inside our borders, why—"

"No more questions. I have told you why. Live with it or leave. You are not worthy yet of a deeper answer."

"If we can't—"

"I said, enough!" his words were a gusting wind, sucking the air and life from the room.

Rydel's excitement at going to train with the Terma warred with sorrow. Never to see the light of day. To hide. *A knife in the dark.What else did I think becoming a Hidden meant?* He realized he'd been holding out some deep, buried hope that he'd be able to see his mother again.

"Master, can we at least *talk* to them?" Rydel asked bitterly.

"I will not bind your tongue so long as you do not disclose your training or anything about your true identity."

"So pretty much nothing then," Dryan said. "Great."

Master Trinaden gave him a sharp look, but he seemed to overlook some of Dryan's flippant comments of late. Instead, he looked at the dark-haired, blue-eyed boy with a sense of regret in his eyes. "Will we have a problem, Dryan?"

Dryan flushed and bowed his head. "No, Master."

"Good. Gather your things then meet me outside."

Outside, Master waited, a strange lumpy bundle on his back. Rydel thought he knew what the oblong shaped package was, or at least what was in it, yet he was afraid to get his hopes up. He sensed the same from his brothers.

They traveled in silence, wearing their new masks. It felt strange, hiding. The cloth mask fit snuggly, hiding all but his eyes. Rydel looked over at his brothers and saw only their different colored gazes. They wore their traditional hidden-in-training gray-green clothes that blended with the forest about them.

"These feel weird," Dryan said, rubbing at the mask. "Ugh, they itch too. Why do I have to hide my face? I mean, you Hadrian it makes perfect sense. That ugly mug of yours definitely deserves a mask. I figure Master was just being kind letting it go and not telling you all this time. My face, however, should be showcased to the world."

Hadrian grunted. "The real question is: can we also put a muzzle on you? I think it'd complete the ensemble and really save us some headaches, right, Rydel?" Hadrian nudged Rydel in the ribs.

Rydel was distracted though. Usually, their banter made him smile, and he occasionally joined in. As they slowed, the vast city of Eldas opened up before them. Lights glowed like fireflies in the trees above. He realized his heart was pounding. Memories of his childhood, of leaving, returned in a rush, and he shoved them down.

"Enough," Master Trinaden said. "We're here."

Master led them to an enormous glen. The trees were giants here—ancient watchers that reached for the sky above. Rydel felt them hum with life, sentient beings telling of the generations of elves that had come before.

High above, Rydel spotted hints of the famed city of Eldas. Resplendent structures made of purple heartwood were suspended in the weighty boughs, seamlessly constructed into the trees. Walkways crisscrossed overhead and muted lights continued to pulse alluringly, giving it all an enchanted feel. The pounding in his heart grew along with a strange pull. A longing. Eldas... This was his home. Home of the elves. His mother. He was so close, and yet he was supposed to remain silent, a mystery. How could he? Rydel thought he'd forget. He'd been told to forget. Unfortunately, he couldn't. He wouldn't. No matter what Master said, if he found a chance, he'd find her.

Rydel's warrior's eyes took in the little details before him. The green grass of the glen was close-cropped, worn down to near dirt by countless feet. Then the green magic of the elves would make it grow again tomorrow, only to be shorn down anew.

On the grounds, elves clashed in a dazzling display. Terma he knew, the most elite warriors of the Great Kingdom of Leaf. The Terma spared in a dozen little rings. In the center of each ring, two combatants with dulled metal training swords collided. Each one looked more like a dancer, twisting, turning, ducking swift strikes and returning the strokes effortlessly. Agile and powerful blows made the glen ring with the sound of clashing and occasional laughter and chatter.

They stopped at the far edge of the glade.

"This looks like fun," Hadrian said. "May we, Master?"

Trinaden raised an eyebrow. "You'll want these I suspect." Pulling the big bundle off his shoulder, he loosened a few strings, rolling it out onto the ground. Lying there were three swords in leather sheaths. "Their edges are as sharp as a drekkar's claws. Swords are weapons, not toys." They each waited, giddy with anticipation. "Well, what are you waiting for?"

Though there were three, they shoved and pushed one another to get at the long-awaited prize. Rydel was slower. It wasn't the leafblade, but it was something. Taking a sword each, they pawed their newfound treasure. Trinaden inclined his head and they ran off towards the waiting Terma when Rydel felt iron-like fingers grip his arm, holding him back. "Master?"

"Rydel," Trinaden said, his eyes hard and mysterious. "Remember, you are not like them. Mingle, learn, but do not get too close. You risk them if you do. You are a blade too sharp to hold. Remember that. Do not make the same mistake I did."

I did...? Again, the dark haunting look flashed across Trinaden's normally steely expression. Rydel nodded, confused, and Trinaden waved him off and he joined up with his brothers.

As they neared, a big elf greeted them.

"Greetings," he said with an elegant bow and a charming smile. *Their leader,* Rydel knew immediately judging by his confident stance and smooth, deep voice of practiced authority. Aside from Master, he was perhaps the biggest elf Rydel had ever seen, easily as big as Hadrian, maybe bigger. Green plated armor fit his huge frame snuggly, bulging at his chest and arms. On his wrists, two golden bracers were clasped, signifying his rank. "I'm Aladar, the Commander of the Terma. High Commander Elinar told me you'd be coming. We're glad to have you."

Before they could respond Aladar shouted, "Elisaria, Cylar!"

A hawk-nosed elf with dark eyes and blonde-almost-white hair approached wearing bronze bracers. Third-in-command, Rydel knew. The haughty imperious stare rankled Rydel as the man eyed them up and down like mangy dogs carrying something contagious. Aladar clapped the slender elf on the shoulder. "This is my third in command, Cylar."

The elf only snorted.

Aladar growled, "Respect, Cylar." Cylar only curled his lip. Then Aladar turned just as a loud cheer went out from a nearby ring. A female elf broke from the ring to a round of clapping and jubilations, clearly the victor. "Ah, perfect timing. This is Elisaria." Rydel noticed the silver bracers on her wrists. "My second in command and granddaughter to the High Commander himself. Elisaria these are our new friends—"

Aladar paused waiting for Rydel and his brothers to fill the gap with their names.

Pulling a cloth that had been tucked inside the folds of her armor, Elisaria wiped her face and filled the awkward silence, "They can't tell you their names, Aladar—weren't you listening to grandfather? They're not allowed to tell us, are you?"

"Why's that?" Cylar asked contemptuously.

"Because they're different. They're Hidden."

Whispers rushed among all those who were near enough to hear, and even nearby fighters stopped their clashes and turned their keen, pointed ears to the conversation.

"Ah, we're not supposed to know that, are we?" Elisaria asked. "But we'd have to be pretty foolish not to have heard the stories," She looked directly at Rydel and despite all his training, he felt sweat break out slightly at his temples.

Rydel wasn't sure he liked the way she looked at him and it seemed only *him*. Her eyes pierced him and seemed to ask: *who are you?*

"Well, the lady has the right idea and good questions," Hadrian broke in smoothly. "But truthfully, we are not Hidden. Not yet at least."

"No—you're not quite like him, are you?" Elisaria said, looking at Master Trinaden who watched from afar with his muscular arms crossed before his body. Like them, he wore a black mask that covered all but his eyes. Looking at him now it was difficult to even catch his frame as the grand hando cloak made the tree he leaned on look a part of him. "He has death in his eyes. You..." she looked Hadrian and Dryan up and down who stood cockily, "you're just boys."

Dryan snapped back, "Brave words coming from a girl. Why don't you back that up?"

Elisaria raised a brow. "You think you could take me?"

"Take you?" Dryan asked, with a hint of a lecherous sneer that raised the hair on Rydel's neck and made his fist tremble. He was ready to smack his brother, but Dryan changed his tone and replied, "Any one of us could do that with our arms bound. The question is, how sound is your pride? Can it withstand being defeated in front of your pathetic peers?"

"My pride?" Elisaria said. "It can withstand a boy champing at the bit to prove himself. A boy who looks like a toddler beside his peers."

The expertly placed taunt, as Rydel expected, found its mark like an arrow hitting the broadside of a barn. Dryan snapped. With a cry, Dryan unsheathed his blade in a whirlwind and crossed the distance between him and Elisaria in a flash. Cylar's blade cleared its sheath as well, though he was too slow. Rydel, however, was quickest. He'd sensed this coming and pulled his dagger free as well as his training sword. Normally, he wasn't as fast as his brother, but need propelled him. Both blades crashed down, and he held the two—Cylar and Dryan in a locked parry. Only then did he glare at Dryan, "Brother," he warned. "This is not our code." *Strength is life, weakness death,* was the first of the Hidden's three codes. But a quick second and equally tantamount code was: *fight only when necessary.*

Dryan's gaze was all fire and brimstone behind his black mask. Then he shook himself, and his breathing slowed and he pulled back, sheathing his blade.

Cylar scowled. Looking at the elf, Rydel thought the third-in-command looked like Dryan's inverse cousin. Where Dryan's hair was raven-black, Cylar's was almost white, and where Dryan had white-blue eyes, Cylar's were hateful obsidian stones. Even their words carried the same bile-filled contempt. "That's right. Keep your rabid hound in line," Cylar said with a sneer, but he didn't sheath his blade. "Attack Elisaria again and I'll put him down like the mangy dog he is."

Rydel didn't want to tell the elf he'd spared both Elisaria and Cylar's own life. He'd parried Dryan's blade a good second before Cylar's—the Terma's parry would never have arrived. But he kept his tongue, seeing wisdom in not fanning the already rising flames.

Elisaria sighed, side-stepping Cylar to stand on her own. "For the hundredth time, I don't need your unrequested gallantry, Cylar. I can handle myself." The way she said it, Rydel didn't doubt it for a second.

A deep booming laugh from Aladar, the huge elf, shook the woods and diffused the mounting tension. Raising his hands Aladar smiled a broad, charming smile, "Please please, no need to bandy words when we can bandy swords. After all, we're all brothers and sisters beneath the eyes of the Great Spirit. If we're done squabbling, shall we begin our training?"

"I still don't get it. If we don't allow the guard to train with us, why should we allow them?" Cylar asked.

Aladar shrugged. "Why not? I've never known you to turn down a challenge, brother."

"Please," Rydel interjected. "Allow us a match to prove ourselves. We won't disappoint." His felt his brothers amusement behind him, though he kept his own features neutral. They might not have been enemies, and he sensed their threats as harmless boasts; all the same, Rydel was eager, almost impatient to prove himself, and they didn't need to know anything until their blades met.

"Fine," Elisaria said. "Choose your opponent." She gave Rydel a hard stare as if readying herself.

Then Rydel swiveled, directing the point of his blade to Aladar. "I challenge you." Rydel felt the heat of Elisaria's eyes, glaring at him and judging him.

"Please, brother, allow me," Hadrian said, stepping forth. "This one is more my size after all."

Dipping his head, Rydel acquiesced.

The two squared off. Hadrian, who was a giant, almost looked small, or at least average, next to the commander of the Terma. Aladar grinned easily and withdrew a massive sword looked more suitable for fighting giants than elves. "Are you certain you wish to fight me first, brother? You might want to work your way up, no offense intended."

"No offense taken," Hadrian said coolly, then launched himself forward.

Their swords clashed, sparks flying. It sent a ring and a reverberation through all those watching. Again the titans clashed, muscles straining. Surprise rippled through the Terma and all in attendance.

Elves began to filter from the other circles to watch the battle.

Aladar's face was one of strain and concentration.

"He's holding Commander Aladar's parry!" A Terma shouted in disbelief.

"That's impossible," said another.

Then Aladar bellowed, pushing forward. The parry broke and Hadrian dodged a cut to his head and struck with a slice to Aladar's torso. Aladar, much faster than expected for his bulk, brought his foot to Hadrian's chest—sending the young elf sprawling. The fall, however, turned into a graceful tuck and roll, something they'd practiced endlessly, and Hadrian was back on his feet, so fast it was questionable if he'd ever fallen. Another series of rapid strikes were met with easy parries by Aladar, but Rydel saw, despite the Terma's stoic face, a vein was pulsing at his temple and strain was beginning to show.

Then Aladar cried out, shoving off Hadrian's sword from a parry, pulling free a side-sword at his belt. With a swooping circular strike, he parried, then cut. The small sword flashed.

They pulled away.

Aladar was breathing a little harder than when they'd started, but not much. Hadrian, on the other hand, was breathing as evenly as if he'd gone for a moonlit stroll. Yet at his waist, his green and gray clothes were cut, and he was bleeding from a hand-length wound on his muscled torso. Hadrian touched it with a finger. His green eyes the only thing visible behind his black mask as he eyed the blood as if surprised. It didn't seem like Hadrian to miscalculate the distance of his opponent's blade; yet Aladar's sword was a hand length longer than even most greatswords—getting inside the reach of that behemoth was a feat in itself. Still, Rydel thought, it wasn't like Hadrian. He knew his brother was up to something.

The young commander of the Terma grinned and the other Terma broke into excited whispers. "You are a worthy opponent, young Hidden," Aladar proclaimed loudly. "In time, we might even be a match."

"Ah, yes," Hadrian replied. "Unfortunately, we are not a match."

Rydel knew that smile from his ever-smiling brother. It was wider, cockier. A smile he'd seen brandished against him when Hadrian had the edge; and Rydel saw what the others, aside from Dryan and Master Trinaden, did not. Hadrian wasn't testing the elf's prowess. A test was necessary when sizing up an opponent of equal strength. Hadrian wasn't doing that. He'd sized up the elf the moment he'd seen him from a distance. Instead, he was toying with Aladar.

Elisaria came to his side, crossing her arms. "It seems your friend has lost."

"Perception is a tricky thing," Rydel answered.

"He's cut, is he not? While Aladar remains unharmed. The show is over."

Rydel only shrugged. "Perception is a tricky thing," he repeated, eyeing her sidelong. "Besides, I've always preferred the second act."

The woman, her stunning, graceful features fixed ahead, only smiled. At his wit? At his bravado? It was just a bare twitch of her perfect pink lips, and he wasn't sure of the implication, but it made his heart thunder.

Meanwhile, all those in attendance watched the two big elves, waiting.

Hadrian raised his blade. "Again?"

"Are you an idiot?" Cylar asked, gawking, "He won, you lost. Can't you see that, you silly swaggering bu—"

The commander of the Terma's brows furrowed and he raised a hand, stalling his third-in-command. "Cylar's crude and foolhardy, alas he's often right. As it stands you are no match for me. I do not wish to harm you anymore. Admit defeat, brother, and we can train together. I'm sure there is much we can learn and teach you."

Scratching his chin, Hadrian yawned. "A commendable offer, *brother,*" Hadrian said, amused. Rydel knew Hadrian only thought himself brothers with two elves, and Aladar wasn't one of them. "Consider myself duly warned. Again?"

"So be it." Aladar charged, moving like a rockslide of muscle and steel. Despite his size, the commander of the Terma crashed from stance to stance, slashing, parrying, riposting, and in-between throwing effortless kicks and elbows. Awe-inspiring advanced moves and stances rolled out of the elf. Breathtaking as it was, Hadrian blocked, dodged, or dipped every strike. If he wasn't fighting Hadrian, the Terma would have seemed unstoppable. As it was, Rydel saw the end approaching swiftly. Aladar cried out, sweat draining down his face as he delivered a sweeping overhead strike.

Hadrian side-stepped it by a hair, as if watching it in slow-motion, planted his foot onto the sword—making it dip and stick into the hard-packed earth. Aladar pulled on the blade, but to no avail, as if it was embedded in stone. Hadrian took the moment to smack Aladar's hands with the flatter edge of his blade in a smooth motion, then circled his body and elbowed Aladar in the gut. Aladar gusted air from his lungs, releasing his grip and stumbling back from the strike. Circling with the strike—a strike without power or hurt, only intended to create space—Hadrian kicked the fallen blade up to his other hand, catching the twirling steel in midair, twirled, and leveled both to the commander of the Terma.

Aladar didn't have a cut or scrape on him. He looked dazed at the sudden turn of events. Nevertheless, it was over—the skill of Hadrian so swiftly and aptly shown that a hushed silence settled over all in attendance.

Save for Elisaria, who clapped slowly at Rydel's side. The rest of the elves remained stunned.

Aladar slowly shook himself, rubbing his smarting hands. Hadrian flipped one of the blades around smoothly and handed it back to Aladar. The commander stared at it, took it, then grinned wildly and clasped Hadrian warmly. "Well done, brother. Welcome to Terma's training grounds. You are free to train with whomever you wish." He barked a few orders and Terma surged forth, eager to take part and learn from the three hidden-in-training.

Cylar cursed, spitting on the ground and slinking back into the crowds. Elisaria watched through the throng. Rydel made his way to her. She bowed her head in greeting. "Welcome," she said.

"Thank you," he answered, then looked to where Cylar had left. Rydel nodded in that direction. "What's with your friend? What'd we do to him?"

"Don't mind Cylar. He just... doesn't like newcomers."

Rydel grunted. "Who put the nettle in his shirt? You'd think I kicked his hound with the way he looks at us." Even now, as the elves milled, he caught a glimpse of the white-haired elf who shot him a final glare before turning to train with another Terma.

"Cylar's a kicked hound himself," she said slowly, a sympathetic strain in her eyes. "He... was once Commander. Yet when one of the sentries on his watch wandered too close to Drymaus Forest, the young sentry was killed by a drekkar. It wasn't his fault. The sentry was young, new, but Cylar still blamed himself. It doesn't help that the High Commander is his father as well. Treats him more harshly than anyone else. I wouldn't worry about him." Rydel nodded, looking back over the camp. Elves were beginning to break up—Terma asking to spar Dryan and Hadrian. The towering trees watched over him, and a wind of change stirred inside Rydel. Dozens of elves watched him from a distance and his exchange with their second-in-command. They seemed hesitant to approach, though he wasn't sure why. "So," Elisaria said, with a sly grin, "I have to ask. Are you as fast as your big friend?"

"Faster," Rydel admitted.

"You're their leader then?"

"We are brothers, equals."

"Modesty suits you," she said. "The others, not so much."

"We have our different strengths. My brothers make up where I fall short, and I... well, I'd like to think I do the same for them."

"Then I'd like to see your strengths," Elisaria replied with a flirtatious twist to her lips. "And your weaknesses," she said boldly. "Will you spar with me?"

Rydel grinned. "It would be my honor."

A ring was made, and their duel commenced. Hefting the blade in his hand, he realized it was the same weight as the wooden training swords they'd been using. Heavy dense heartwood—which transitioned to his new metal weapon feel almost seamless. Still, he slowly built up speed.

Rydel discovered that Elisaria was fast, faster than any elf he'd seen before, aside from his brothers and Master Trinaden, and where she wasn't as strong as Aladar, or as nimble as he'd seen Cylar move, she was their strengths combined. In a way, she reminded Rydel of himself. Parrying a blow that was meant for his right arm, he flicked her sword back with more strength than before and her eyes tightened. Then he gave another strike—this time, twisting his hands inward to increase and breathing out in a sharp burst to increase his power. Elisaria raised her blade, planting her feet. The power, however, was more than she anticipated. He watched as she absorbed the blow with clenched teeth, barely able to redirect the strike and hold her blade.

Elisaria recovered, shaking her hand as if she'd slammed her blade into rigid steel. He knew the feeling having suffered the same strike from Master Trinaden when he'd first been taught. Her hands would likely feel numb and tingly for a day. "What was that?" She asked in an accusing tone, sheathing her blade.

Rydel feigned ignorance. "What was what?"

"That move... Don't play dumb." Even as she said it, though she still sounded annoyed, there was a sly smile on her pink lips and a light in her eyes. As if she was excited.

"I'm not sure what you're talking about," he lied.

Elisaria sniffed and turned, leaving.

As she did, his heart fell—and then she turned and glanced back over her shoulder, and he saw a quirk to her lips. Rydel's heart floated in his chest. That night, after they had returned to Trinaden's little cottage on the border of Eldas, all Rydel could think about was Elisaria. She consumed his mind. That smile she'd flashed him as she'd been leaving lingered in his dreams. That she'd known he'd been hiding something made him excited. Somehow, he knew she wasn't done with him either. The next day, after defeating a dozen Terma, Elisara found him again. "He's mine," she declared, and the others made a ring about them.

They clashed once more, swords and bodies dancing in a beautiful rhythm in which Rydel lost himself to when—

"Don't toy with me," Elisaria said as she dove back from a strike. "I know you're slowing your strikes intentionally."

"You wish me to go full out?" Rydel asked.

"I wish to see what you're capable of—this isn't it."

A second later, Rydel crossed the distance. Elisaria's eyes flashed wide, barely registering his speed gained from countless hours of sprints with hundreds of pounds of rocks on his back. Agile as ever, she raised her sword in the nick of time. Instead, Rydel swiped her feet from beneath her. She fell. Before she landed on her back, Rydel slammed his sword into the ground and caught her lightly.

She stared up at him, searching his eyes for a long moment, still panting. Rydel's breathing was even, but as she stared into his eyes, his arm cradling her body which felt light, and warm, he felt his own breathing quicken. "What are you?" Elisaria asked.

The way she said it made him wince as if struck.

"I didn't..." she began.

A sudden urge filled him looking into her eyes. Her breaths came quicker, chest rising and falling. She was so warm in his hands but—

Then he remembered.

They had an audience. Dozens of Terma watched them, judging. From them, he sensed their varying emotions as he held their second-in-command. In that moment, he felt different and realized though they'd been welcomed, Rydel wasn't truly one of them. When they moved about the training grounds, whispers always followed, or the deferential looks from Aladar, or the hateful glares from Cylar. He was different. *They* were different. Master was right. He was caught up in these thoughts, lost when—

Elisaria kicked his feet out from under him and he collapsed like a felled oak. She rolled to her feet and grabbed his blade that had been sticking from the ground, and aimed it at his throat. Rydel still shaken by his thoughts, looked up at her in a daze. Scarlet hair tumbled down to her shoulders, highlighting her beautiful face. Her sky-blue eyes looked at him with brimming mirth. "You've finally lost. I was beginning to think you weren't mortal or an elf. How does it feel to be beaten?"

Rydel's managed a laugh. "By you? Practically an honor." Then thought, *I would gladly lose a hundred times just to be so near.*

She rolled her eyes. "Come now. You already lost, you don't need to ply me with sweet words. I won't run you through, I promise." They continued, sparing deep into the night until his brothers pulled him away and he left with a smile on his lips and thoughts of her on his mind.

Weeks went by like this, training with Elisaria with every free moment he or she had. If he didn't search her out, she would find him. Words weren't necessary, yet over time he wanted to ask her things. A desire to know her, to ask her questions about her life burgeoned inside him. Always as they would pause he would feel the sensation growing... but then he would remember his Master's words. *Don't get too close.* Instead, they'd finish, tired and slicked with sweat—going until Trinaden or his brothers practically pulled him away. Each time, however, he'd wait for that moment when she'd look back and flash him that same smile of hers—a smile that felt just his.

None of his brother's teasing could take that smile from him.

One day, a month into their training, Rydel sat under a tree, sweat straining from his face after sparring an endless stream of willing combatants. No matter how many he seemed to lay down, a dozen more took their place, and he admired them for it. Elisaria found him, an apple in hand, and plopped down at his side wordlessly. She offered him the red fruit, and he stared at it uncertainly. "It won't bite," she said, confused.

He took it slowly, then lifted his mask slowly.

"Why the mask?" She asked, interrupting him.

Rydel froze, apple halfway to his mouth. Master's words came back to him, unbidden and he echoed them, "'To be a Hidden means to be a knife in the dark, nameless and quiet, nothing more, nothing less.'"

She looked at him with an arched brow. "That... doesn't answer my question."

Rydel held her gaze then they laughed together, and he conceded with a nod. "No, I suppose it doesn't. It was Master's idea. He says Hidden have many enemies, or we will. My mask keeps my identity secret, so anyone I care about will be kept safe from those who would wish to do me harm and discover more about me or my whereabouts."

Slowly she nodded. "That makes more sense." He still held the apple. "Eat," she said, gesturing.

The mask covered from the bridge of his nose down, a hanging cloth tied in the back. Lifting the mask just enough to expose his mouth, he took a bite and an explosion of flavor made his eyes nearly water.

"So you do eat," Elisaria remarked. "Surprises never end around you."

Rydel continued to chew, savoring the crunch and tart flesh of the apple. The texture was so unlike anything he'd ever experienced. The gruel was pasty and bland. This was pure bliss. He never thought the texture of something alone could be so delightful. "This... this is remarkable. This is what an apple tastes like, all this time?"

"Are you saying... You've never... eaten an apple?"

Judging by her baffled expression and tone, you would think Rydel had just announced that he enjoyed eating dung, or that he was the Ronin of wind himself. "Never," he replied with a shrug. "You wouldn't like what I normally eat. This..." His mouth still tingled from the sensation. "This is magic, surely. Farhaven be blessed," he uttered in prayer.

She laughed thinking he was joking. "You're a funny thing," Elisaria said, shaking her head in amusement. "Why have you never tasted an apple before?"

Master Trinaden was in his usual place, leaning against the trunk of a tree as Dryan and Hadrian spared with a dozen Terma at the same time. Trinaden watched impassively. "Master says we must harden ourselves to all things, to all temptations."

"All... temptations?" Elisaria asked, lifting a brow.

Heat suffused Rydel's cheeks and he breathed a slow, even breath as he'd been taught. It was a trick to release the emotions building in him, though now it did little good. Wisely, he opted for silence, watching Dryan nimbly roll between a Terma's legs, then run up the blade of another, kneeing the elf in the face. Hadrian threw two more elves against a tree-trunk.

"You're not like your brothers," she remarked. "You aren't truly brothers, are you?"

Rydel felt a spike of resentment at this. "We are brothers, more than blood—bound by a fate you could never understand."

Elisaria looked taken aback by his harsh words and tone, if only for a moment. "I meant no offense, truly. I'm sorry if I struck a nerve. I meant only that... Well, you're different. Not size of course. You're big though your one brother is practically a draft horse. He can nearly look our big oaf Aladar eye to eye. And the little one, while handsome, looks part dark-elf, if those still existed. His hair and frozen eyes would make you distant cousins at best."

"Blood means nothing," Rydel said softly, taking another bite of apple.

"It means *something*."

"Does it?" He asked, looking to her, handing the apple back. "A child can't choose their parents or their siblings. We are different. Our brotherhood is a choice. Bound by hardship, by sacrifice. What we are is thicker than any bond borne out of happenstance."

Elisaria seemed to ponder this a moment, tapping her pink lips in thought, then offered, "True, though that doesn't explain the bond between a father and his daughter, or a mother and her son..." Staring ahead, he felt her gaze on him, searching him, testing him. Somehow this conversation felt more akin to a sparring match, and he had a sinking feeling he was losing. Still, he guarded his expression when she mentioned the bond of a mother and son, while his insides churned with unrest. "I've seen a mother willing to sacrifice herself for her son at the drop of a hat. Surely you can't call that bond circumstantial and trite."

For a moment, Rydel debated his answer, then posted the safest one. He remained silent again, watching his brothers.

Elisaria sidled closer, handing him the apple once more. "But I wasn't talking about that."

"Then what do you mean?" Rydel felt bad that he sounded snappy, but he knew she was nipping at something close, trying to root out answers, and she knew it too. He could see it on her face.

"You're kinder than them. Gentler."

Rydel chuckled softly. "You're wrong about that."

"Well, at the least, you're less arrogant."

"No offense to my brothers, that's not too hard. Though their pride is well deserved."

Still, Elisaria's eyes searched him. "I don't know what burden is placed on you. But you seem to move with a weight on your shoulders, always cautious and considerate. I know you'd do anything for them."

"You know a lot," he said, eyeing her sidelong, then gave a small smile.

Elisaria smiled back, and it made his heart thunder. "I know enough. I can't quite figure out what eats at you, though. They might have covered it up, but you haven't. I can see something from your past, something maybe in your training. It pains you daily, doesn't it? You can speak to me. I won't tell a soul."

Rydel didn't like how close she was getting with her truths. He felt his heart harden, but her hand touched his shoulder, gently. Slowly, he turned to look at her. There was no malice in her eyes. Elisaria was fierce to her core. She had a fighter's spirit, and yet in this moment, she let down her guard, for him. "Take off your mask," she said. He knew she meant it in more ways than one. Slowly, she reached for it, touching the clasp and—

Trinaden's words echoed in his ears, *'Remember, you are not like them. Mingle, learn, but do not get too close. You risk them if you do. You are a blade, too sharp to hold. Remember that.'*

Expelling a heavy breath, Rydel rose. He looked back and saw the hurt on Elisaria's face. She had been exposed, removing the armor that guarded her own hard heart, asking for him to do the same and he had denied her. A pain stabbed at his chest as he looked down at her. And yet, Trinaden's words held some deeper truth he couldn't understand quite yet. *You risk them if you do.* "I have to go," he said, and she nodded softly, looking away and he saw tears on her cheek.

Ignoring every instinct and muscle in his body, Rydel pulled himself away from that tree, dropping the apple on the ground. He wasn't being selfish or afraid. Was he?

When he returned to the Terma fighting grounds the next day, Elisaria avoided him. Had she approached, he wasn't sure if he'd be able to deny her again. Yet the offer was never made. He'd burned her and now she feared the fire of his denial. Rydel couldn't blame her and he hated himself for it. That night, when they returned to their hut–tucked deep in the forest—as they did every night, Trinaden placed a hand on his shoulder, and somehow he knew his Master knew. As they made meals and cleaned up, he was snappier at Dryan and Hadrian, though his brothers suffered his torment good naturedly.

Each day they returned to the Terma training grounds for the next months. Each time he'd see Elisaria and she'd avoid him and so he lost himself to the sword, to his training. On the third month of their training with the Terma, Trinaden announced they had learned all they could from their elite elven brothers and sisters and it was time to say goodbye.

They walked in silence to the Terma camp—a good dozen mile walk to the grand clearing. A familiar walk. One that Rydel had looked forward to each morning. Each day, both sad and hopeful for Elisaria's reaction. When they reached the clearing, the Terma were waiting like they had been on the first day, gathered in a large crowd with their commander at their head. Bowing they made their formal goodbyes, thanking Commander Aladar who warmly embraced Rydel and Hadrian. Dryan remained distant and aloof as if elevated above the green-lacquered elves. Trinaden forced his hand and Dryan made a reluctant, shallow bow. When it was time to leave, however, Rydel lingered.

The other Terma turned and left except one.

Elisaria remained behind.

Rydel's heart hammered staring at her, but then she too turned and left. Heavy-hearted, Rydel waited, but when it was clear she wasn't coming back, he left. When he reached the edge of the Terma training ground, seeing Dryan and Hadrian far ahead on their return home, something flew out of the air. Rydel felt as much as heard the soft whistle and caught it. *An... apple?*

Elisaria came out from behind a tree with a small smile. "You're leaving," she said. Was it a question? A statement?

Rydel swallowed. He could only nod.

The beautiful elf had an apple of her own. She bit into it, the juice dripping from her mouth and some spilling down her pink lips and off her chin. Elisaria wiped her chin clean with her wrist and leaned against the tree. "You know you've changed us," she said, then gestured back over her shoulder to the Terma training ground.

"How so?"

"We used to think we were so superior. That nothing could harm us. That our training had made us not just special but somehow... more. Better than others. The best even. You've nicked that armor, exposed the flaws in their thinking. Some despise you for it. Hate you for showing their weakness. That even being a Terma, with all our skill and prowess, still, there's someone better out there. I think that scares them. It makes them feel... normal. For elves whose whole lives they've felt different, special, and better—it's not a great feeling."

Rydel smiled. She was special. "And what do you think?"

"I'm not going to lie. I felt that smugness too. Now, I'm glad for the humbling." Elisaria took another small crunching bite, leaving her tree and drawing near. "Do you know why?"

Rydel remained frozen by her gaze, locked in place. He'd stared down Trinaden's lightning blade, and countless elves flashing steel, but those green eyes... they stole his words and arrested him. Made him feel more sluggish and numb than he'd ever felt in all his life. Still, he managed to shake his head. "Why?"

"Because I realize we're not better. Not just the Terma—sure we're faster and stronger than most. But we're not better. I can see in your eyes, you see the same. You don't view yourself as above, as superior to all else, even if you have every reason to. You've never even been beaten."

He laughed. "You don't know Master."

"If that was true, then why are your brothers so different?"

"They train for themselves, at least I know my middle brother does."

"And you don't?"

"If I did, I wouldn't be here." She looked at him puzzled, and he explained. "If I had to view my training as purely a means to make myself

41

the strongest, I don't think I'd survive. I'm not strong enough, or perhaps selfish enough for such a self-absorbed goal."

"Then what is your goal?"

"Farhaven," he admitted. "I love these woods, the elves, my..." he thought about his mother but pushed it aside, controlling his expression. "I love Eldas, deeply. But something in me knows that there's so much more out there. So much more is at stake."

"You are a rarity. An elf who doesn't view Eldas as tantamount to all else?"

"I wish to see the world," Rydel confessed. "I've read books on them." His eyes panned north as if he could see the images that flashed in his mind's eye. "The gleaming mirrors and glass columned spires of Vaster, city of sun. The trading city of Cloudfel, home to all manner of people—"

Just then, Elisaria interrupted him with a gleam in her eyes, stepping forward eagerly, "—or the sprawling desert city of Covai, city of flesh— teeming with man and beast under the hot sun—"

Rydel grinned behind his mask, snapping back, "—Narim, the great city of moon, half above the land half below, shining like a turquoise gem—"

With each new city, Elisaria took another step closer until they were paces away. "—Farbs, the Great Kingdom of Fire, where the fiery incantations of the Reavers light up the desert's night sky." She gripped his arm as if was simply instinct, lost in the thought of grand worlds beyond their own. "Light and heavens, can you see them too? I wish to go more than anything." Elisaria was breathless, her eyes gleaming.

Lost in her emerald gaze, he smiled and wished to tell her he wanted to take her, to travel the world with her, but he could only hold her gaze. "I will go one day," Rydel said. "When I pass my trials, I will leave Eldas."

"Why?"

"It's my purpose. To protect not just our people, but all of Farhaven. To that end, I must be strong."

Still, she didn't drop her hand and continued. "You're the same as me, aren't you? Eldas can't stand alone any longer. The world needs to unite— the Great Kingdoms uniting as one. Secluded behind the Gates of Eldas will only see our slow demise, our decay. Not to mention, we have so much to learn still. So much the rest of Farhaven has yet to teach us." He wanted to agree, to shout his affirmation but he only held her eyes, that breath of space between them. "Will you take me with you?"

Again, Trinaden's words hammered into him. *You will hurt anyone you get too close to. You are a knife too sharp to hold.* Rydel cared for Elisaria. More than he had cared for anyone. Behind his mask, she could only read his eyes. And again, letting the knife into his chest as if plunging it inward with his own hands, he remained silent.

This seemed enough answer for Elisaria, who nodded slowly, softly. Hurt registered in her eyes, but a part of her seemed resigned—as it had been a last, hopeful ditch effort. Slowly, she backed away. When she reached the tree where she'd thrown the apple he called out to her, unable to help himself.

She paused, looking at him. "Why do you like me?" Elisaria asked. "Do you like me?"

Rydel's tongue was thick in his throat as his words came like a flood, *because you're beautiful enough to take my breath away each time I see you. Because you're clever, funny, enigmatic. Because of your smile. Because of the way I want to be around you, always and anywhere. Because I can't stop thinking about you, and I don't want to.* These and a thousand other sentiments bombarded his brain like arrows pincushioning a haystack, yet when he opened his mouth nothing came out. An insect trilled in the bushes, and the wind brushed the boughs, rustling cloak and leaf. When the silence stretched too long, Elisaria nodded slowly as if again this was answer enough and she spoke instead, "Then if you're too afraid, I will tell you. I like you because while other elves seek to dominate me, see me as a trophy, something to win or woe, another conquest... You see me as something else. Those eyes look at me with something I've never felt before. You're different." She smiled sadly. "Even if you're too afraid to show it, or perhaps know it yourself. *That's* why I like you."

Rydel's breathing was staggered, his every muscle tense and coiled. Slowly Elisaria nodded, biting her lip, and then she turned. He called to her back, "If it helps, I doubt any but three arrogant boys in all of Farhaven can make a nick in that armor of yours."

"Not three, just one," she said softly.

Rydel narrowed his gaze at her. Did... He didn't think she meant real armor now. Again, Elisaria resumed walking. As always, he waited for that moment she would turn and look back at him over her shoulder flashing him that smile that was only his. At least he could take that with him. Please, at least that. Only this time, she didn't. Elisaria continued, blending back into the woods and then was gone.

Rydel looked down and realized he still had the apple in his hand. Howling in anger and frustration, at his own folly and uselessness, Rydel threw the apple with all his might, watching it burst upon a nearby tree. Then, as his rage slowly subsided making way for his sorrow, he stood alone in the clearing. Heart like a stone in his chest, he returned home.

He thought about Elisaria and their talk for days. Their training with Trinaden resumed in full, and the days with the Terma slowly faded into memory. Still, he thought about her. Weeks, then months, then a year and still the pain and his folly remained.

Then a day came when he forgot his father and his mother's face. That day, he cried and he didn't stop crying. He didn't hear a leaf crack or twig snap. His brothers were too good for that now, but he sensed the elf's presence anyway and he looked up, seeing Hadrian.

Hadrian was even taller now as they entered their seventeenth summer. They were all big for elves—tall and lean. Dryan had grown too, though he was still the shortest. Even he, though, was like a boiled piece of leather, stripped of all fat and twice as tough. "I've forgotten them," he sobbed to Hadrian behind his mask. He could say no more but no more was needed as Hadrian put his arm around him until night faded.

Morning came, and with it, more training. Days came and went, bright green of spring to the blazing heat of summer, summer to the fall—the Relnas Forest's trees shedding their blood-red coats, and fall turning to the crisp bite and deep snows of winter, and on again. They continued to wear their masks, hiding even from each other, so much that Rydel's memory of his brother's faces grew fuzzy. He knew they were aging, and he wondered how much they had changed, how much had he changed. Would he even recognize them anymore? Then he wondered, would he even recognize himself?

Then the day came, at last, the morning of their eighteenth summer.

Master Trinaden came to them. "It is time."

"Time, Master?" Dryan asked. He'd lost his flippant ways, turning harder over the years.

Hadrian, too, had shed some of his casual, boyish humor. Now his voice was deep and serious. "The final test," Hadrian said solemnly.

Rydel had waited impatiently for this day. The Trial of the Forest—their final test.

Master Trinaden inclined his head. "Indeed. Be ready. In the morning, we set out for Drymaus Forest."

That night Rydel and the others slept restlessly. They had heard the tales. Drymaus Forest. A forest full of unspeakable dangers. None but a Hidden had ever entered the woods and left alive.

In the dead of night, Rydel stole out from their little hut—careful not to make any floorboards creak and wake Trinaden or the others—and made his way to Eldas. Something pulled him, guided him and before he knew it he found the Terma encampment—a series of low-lying tents of mossy green and browns camouflaged amid the ancient trees. Rydel snuck past campfires like a shadow, then glided beneath the notice of several sentries keeping watch, to finally find a tent tucked away in the back—a larger green and purple-hued mossy pavilion. Putting his ear to the canvas, he listened. Nothing. Softly, he whispered her name. No answer. Cutting a small slit in the back, he snuck in and found her sleeping form curled on a bed of velvety moss. Rydel's eyes were keen even in the dark and he moved easily to her side. "Elisaria," he whispered gently nudging her.

Elisaria woke in a start, reaching for her dagger.

Rydel clamped his hand over her wrist and another over her mouth so she wouldn't shout out, and felt her muffled scream against his palm. Elisaria's chest heaved. Even in the darkness, he saw she was only in a

45

shift; it was a thin cloth of pearly white, and he saw her outline clearly. He'd never seen her without her armor on and now... If he thought the armor had fit her like a second-skin he'd been mistaken. She was strong, toned, and well-proportioned, and heaving as she was... Rydel turned his face away, but he didn't blush. Urgency and need made his mission too important for modesty. Still, he didn't turn back to face her until she pulled her covers up, slightly. She grabbed a candle and lit it with a fire-starter and when her eyes adjusted to the light she remarked, "You..." she said breathless, "what in the Great Spirits are you doing here?"

"I..." Rydel realized now he hadn't been thinking. He had just acted as if in a trance, as if guided by something more, as if pulled towards her. "I needed to come. Tomorrow... tomorrow I may not be here, and I need you to do something for me."

She looked at him distrustfully, confused, then her eyes widened— hearing the honesty of his words. "What's happening—what is it? What's wrong?" The urgency and fear in her voice tore at him. He'd thought she didn't care, that he'd broken her trust but he was wrong.

"Tomorrow I head to Drymaus Forest."

"No..." she breathed. "No, gods. Not even he would make you do something so reckless. That's a death sentence!"

"It is my final task. I must."

"Don't," she said, grabbing his arm.

"Listen," he replied, shaking his head, "I don't have much time and I can't waste it arguing. I know I don't deserve this, I know I wronged you... but I need you to do me a favor. I need you to deliver a message."

"A message? To whom? I thought you weren't allowed to have any ties, any... temptations?" He realized there was a note of almost jealousy in Elisaria's words, of distrust, and even... something else he couldn't recognize.

Wordlessly, he grabbed her hand and unfurled her clenched fist and deposited his most treasured item. Elisaria examined it in the candlelight. To most, it was just an unassuming little stone with a single character painted on it. The elven character of sha—or *hope* in the common tongue. Her gaze found his, questioning.

Elisaria frowned. "Who gave this to you?"

"My mother," he answered. "It is the only thing I have of hers, the only memory of hers that I still hold. If she's still alive, I want you to find her. Tell her I live. Tell her I still believe—that her son loves her, and I haven't forgotten." Rydel felt his heart clench and the layers of armor he'd carefully cultivated over the years—if only for a moment—crack and fall and he felt raw.

Elisaria saw the look in his eyes, but she shook her head and looked to return the stone, pushing it back into his hands. "I..."

"Rydel. My name is Rydel," he said. "Please, Elisaria. Please do this for me."

Tears formed in her eyes and she tried to wipe them away. "Rydel... Please don't do this. You're going to your death. You know that, don't you? I can't be a part of this. If not delivering the stone means you stay, I'll throw it in the deepest lake and let none find it. Then you can tell her yourself."

Everything inside of him hurt, and Rydel shook his head. "I can't. You don't understand. I... Even this small allowance is breaking every code inside of me as a Hidden."

"Damn the Hidden! You are more than just your code, aren't you? Don't you want to live?" She grabbed his hand, cupping it to her face. "Temptations, *life*. You don't even realize what you're missing. People care about you. *I* care about you. You don't need to throw it away for him."

Rydel looked into her eyes and Trinaden's words returned, sinking into him. *You are more. You can save the world.* Then the man's other words: *don't get too close. You are a blade too sharp to hold.* But Rydel pushed those words aside.With his thumb, he brushed away Elisaria's tears and smiled. "I'm not sure what I am, or what my final destiny is, and I'm not doing it for him. This is for me. I don't know how to explain it, and I know it may seem a fool's errand, but I know that I have to do this. I'm sorry..." he said, and meant it.

Elisaria summoned a tearful smile as if seeing the resolute look in his eyes. "Stubborn fool."

"You haven't answered," he said with a wry smile she couldn't see behind his mask.

She released a shaky breath and nodded, her grip tightening around the small stone.

"I... have to go."

Elisaria grabbed his hand. Hers was strong and rough across the pads as well, but her slender fingers were dwarfed by his own. Rydel felt his heart hammering as he looked back at her. Glowing by the soft candlelight, her face was as stunning as ever—her lips parted slightly as she reached out and touched his mask. He caught her hand, stopping her.

"I..." How did he tell her? He hadn't let anyone see his face in years. Elisaria paused, then slowly continued—the look on her face was gentle, caring, vulnerable—and this time, he didn't stop her. Deftly she untied it and let his black mask slip away to reveal his face. He watched her expression, curious. Elisaria's chest rose and fell, breath quickening as she looked at him. A good sign, he supposed.

"I'm not so hideous then?" Rydel asked, smirking.

"Great Spirits," she breathed, her covers slipping down as her grip went loose, and Rydel—his heart thundering—took her, pulled her close and kissed her deeply, drinking her in. The world swam, time faded as he felt her soft lips pressed against his, felt her tongue exploring his; her body against his, he lost himself to her with the passion of knowing tomorrow may never come.

When she was asleep, he left in the deep night, slipping away—too silent for the sentries, or even for the creatures of Eldas as he made his way back to Master Trinaden's little hut.

In the morning, they found themselves in a clearing just before the tree line of the Drymaus Forest. A lone tree sat in the clearing as if the only thing brave enough to venture close to those shrouded woods; and even it was shriveled and branchless—naked and afraid, quivering its leaves free at what horrors lay within. With his brothers at his side, Master Trinaden addressed them grandly, arms crossed before his chest, "Today you will learn the final code of the Hidden and pass the last of my tribulations. If you survive, you will gain the title of Hidden, if not you will die a warrior's death. However, you will not have the final passing rites of an elf. None will watch you pass or carry your body to the Great Spirit."

"What must we do?" Rydel asked, fear pumping in his veins. He tried to still it and was proud his voice was clear and strong.

"You must enter, find the Hidden Pool, and return with a vial of its sacred water."

The Hidden Pool... Rydel had read about it in a few child's fables. It was a pool in the center of Drymaus Forest. The pool sat at the entrance of what many considered the darkest and forbidding area of Drymaus. Legends said the most terrible of creatures existed there. That it was the home of the dragons...

"Is it true, Master?" Dryan asked. "It exists? *They* exist?"

"I cannot speak of what lives within Drymaus Forest. That is for you to find out, but your objective is simple: find the Hidden Pool and return with proof, alive. The water, as you know, is said to hold magical properties that can heal even the most egregious wound. Return with it and you've passed the final test. Do this and you have achieved the rank of Hidden. This is a task for you alone. You may be brothers, but to be a Hidden, means to be alone."

"Alone? We can't do this together?"

Master Trinaden shook his head. "No. One of you will begin your journey here, at the southern entrance. The next two shall travel with me and I'll deposit you further along, far enough away that your paths will not cross unless you find the heart of the forest."

Alone... Rydel had hoped at least he'd have his brothers. Now his fear grew greater still, but he mastered it, seeing the brave looks on Dryan and Hadrian's faces and knew they were thinking the same thoughts.

Master Trinaden paused, his craggy features growing with concern. Rydel only realized now how his master had aged. The stern-face, never an especially young elf, now bore the signs of time—finer lines splayed at the corners of his eye and mouth. The crease between his furrowed brow had deepened significantly. Though he wore the age with dignity and his usual intimidating air, still... Rydel had always thought their lives were the only sacrifice, now he realized the toll it had taken on Trinaden. His master had given nearly twenty years of his life, never socializing, never wavering, with them every moment. The glassy look in his master's eyes made all the more sense. "I cannot promise you anything. I have done my best to make you into what you are now. You are stronger, faster, harder, more capable than any elf in a thousand years, and this test may still break you." Then Master Trinaden smiled, a rarer than diamond expression for the hardened blademaster. "I wish you the best." With that, he turned his body and opened the path to the dark forest.

The brothers looked at one another.

Rydel took a deep breath. Then he made a motion for his brothers to join him in a small semicircle, out of earshot from Master's keen ears. "I'll go first," he declared.

Dryan snorted, crossing his arms. "And why do you get the glory?"

The bite in his tan-skinned brother's voice surprised Rydel. "If you wish to take the first entrance, brother, I won't stop you. I was only trying to help."

"I know what you are trying to do," Dryan said with a sneer. It wasn't the normal mocking sly look he gave, but one of full derision. The tattoos under his eyes twisted his contorted expression of mockery. "You want to discover the dangers first then you wish to find us and pass on the knowledge."

Hadrian nodded thoughtfully as if this had just occurred to him. "Not a bad idea. But Master said this was a solo venture, did he not?"

"We *are* doing it solo," Rydel replied. "Information is... simply information. We know only tales and fables of these woods. Anything that can help us understand what we're up against and survive will be valuable." Of course, he didn't know how he'd find them, but he'd find a way.

"Seems reasonable enough," Hadrian said.

"No," Dryan snapped. "I'm done with your help."

Rydel and Hadrian both looked at each other as if slapped. "Brother..." Hadrian said, reaching out. "Rydel is only trying to help us."

Dryan slapped the elf's hand away, retreating. "Get off of me!" He yelled. The tan-skinned elf was shaking, trembling with emotion. "Don't you get it? I don't want your help anymore." Again, they looked at one another, baffled. "You don't see it, do you? The way you treat me. Like I'm some sort of burden to bear, a satchel weighing you two down. The guilt, I feel it constantly, wearing me down, gnawing at me." He clutched at his chest as if he claws away the guilt, then he looked up at their expressions and he growled. "Even now! Stop looking at me that way!" He seethed. "I don't want your pity, or worse... that look... that light-cursed look." Dryan's upper lip curled, a crazed light that had always been deep within, surfaced. "You think you're better than me, and perhaps you are for now. But I will be stronger. One day, I will make you both tremble before me." With a snide sneer, Dryan turned away.

"Brother, don't do this," Rydel pleaded.

Dryan looked back and gave him a look that made Rydel freeze—it wasn't the Dryan he'd known, the one he'd saved from the bitter cold, or shared his load, or laughed with or... Then Rydel realized. Or perhaps, this *was* the true Dryan. "I'm not your brother," Dryan said at last, "And I never was." Simple and coldly stated, the words cut Rydel to the core, taking his breath away.

Then Dryan turned on Master Trinaden who stood in the same place, watching with his ever-impassive stony expression, his thick arms crossed before him. Dryan sniffed. "You... I don't need your help either. You're a relic waiting to die."

Trinaden said nothing, yet Rydel saw a slight flinch in the man's craggy face and deep sorrow in those flint-like eyes.

With that, Dryan turned and stalked away—north and towards the woods.

"Dryan!" Rydel called and reached out again, but Hadrian held him back.

The bigger elf shook his head. "He's gone, brother... Let him go."

Rydel knew Hadrian meant it in more ways than one. Tears formed in his eyes and he pressed them down. *Why now of all times?* Aside from his mother, Dryan and Hadrian were the only family Rydel had in this world.And yet, Dryan's words stung—some too close to bitter truth. Had I really thought I was better than him? Deep down, he realized he did.

Hadrian came forward scratching his jaw. "Well, not the goodbye I'd hoped for... But fair well, brother. Watch your back in there, I won't be there to watch it for you."Rydel nodded and they embraced. "Until next we meet," Hadrian said. "And let it be in this life and not the next."

"Until then," Rydel replied and left his brother and Master, knowing he may never see them again. Once he reached the dark edge of the forest, he glanced back to the lone tree and saw they were all gone. "Well, here goes nothing," he whispered to himself. Then he disappeared into the shadowy breath of the forest.

———

The woods collapsed around him. The trees seemed to shuffle in when he wasn't looking, crowding him, suffocating him like black fingers clenching him in their fist—but as he continued, the gnarled oaks, elms, and silveroots thinned. Green grass made a bed in the woods and a golden-white glow replaced the dark aura that had permeated the air. He wondered at the sudden change from dark to light, and first thought it was Drymaus' defense against intruders who sought to plunge and pilfer its wonders. Then he postulated it wasn't Drymaus being evil but good—attempting to warn those too inquisitive souls away for their own safety from the dangers lying within.

A light orange vapor rose from living things and Rydel breathed in. Instantly he felt invigorated, stronger, and faster. *Spark,* he realized. The very air was suffused with magic. Mushrooms dappling the base of a tree were the size of a buckler or tower shield, vines that dangled from above were wrist-thick. Magic made them into giants, and he knew well that bloated mushrooms and melon-sized flowers weren't the only things the growing magic had touched.

As he entered a new kind of glade, he saw the trees soar heavenward, scraping the clouds. None of it held the dark purpose he'd been told. But he didn't question his luck as he continued, passing beneath a tree that—

His hand stuck on something white, and dewy. The white strands looked like taut ropes made into an intricate pattern, and the dew wasn't water, but viscous and glistening. A shadow descended, and the woods darkened. Rydel had a foreboding feeling and suddenly knew what this thing was... Swiftly, he reached for the blade at his side, pulling it free in a rush with his empty left hand as the woods continued to get darker. Every cut snapped the white ropes free but gained a thicker sticky coating on his blade. The stickiness dried almost immediately, turning to glue, hardening and crusting on his blade. Rydel's next strike proved futile as the edge of his blade was gone. His right arm was nearly free, only two more rope-like strands held him in place, but his blade was useless. The sticky substance had turned its once keen edge into little more than a metal baton. Still, he breathed calmly, trying to figure out his next move when... He heard a clicking sound.

Above, he saw it.

An enormous spider made its way down the giant web. Its many black eyes glittered as it spotted its prize. Slavering tendrils dripped from its mandibles that clicked with eager delight at the succulent meal before it.

Trained as he was, Rydel tried to still his racing heart, tried to think, but the monstrous arachnid neared lightning quick. Its bulbous abdomen bounced as it crawled quickly, looking like a boulder tumbling down a hillside. Tugging violently, Rydel tried to rip his arm free, but it felt like trying to wrench free a sword stuck in solid stone. He cried out, and the arachnid quickened its pace, each of its thigh-thick legs skittering across its huge web as it raced towards its prey. Rydel pulled his side dagger free as the creature neared. Then, in the last moment, as its mandibles split and fangs jutted forward, Rydel jammed his dagger into one of the creature's eight black orbed eyes. The giant spider shrieked a horrid clicking cry but slammed him in the head with a leg. The leg felt like a wooden staff to the side of his temple, jarring his thoughts and making the world spin. Clinging to consciousness, Rydel cut at another flashing black leg, and then another, hearing it shriek but it loomed over him still. Through his daze, he saw it lunge, and he barely dipped the snap of its huge mandibles and fangs dripping with poison. Again he jammed his side dagger into another of its eyes, trying to cut deeper but it pulled away wisely. As it did, he cut for his exposed limb—ready to free his wrist rather than die. He knew the small dagger would be worthless against the thick rope-like webbing and would only get caught. Still, sharp as his dagger was—it would take precious moments to saw through his own bone. As he pulled the dagger back, hoping to lop free his wrist in one mighty blow, the spider had recovered and lunged—seeing its opening. It was too late.

Just then, he heard another fierce cry.

A sword darted over his shoulder and plunged into the yawning cavity of the nightmarish spider's slavering mouth. The creature shrieked again, thrashing wildly. The newcomer took another wild strike and Rydel felt his arm free from the sticky webbing and he fell. As his head cleared, the world resolving from a fuzzy nightmare; he looked up to see a green-figured Terma battling against the creature. After another few strikes and shrieks the arachnid, realizing this prize and meal was too costly, and retreated under the flurry of the newcomer's strikes bleeding dark black and purple blood onto the forest floor. With a final, chilling shriek, the creature withdrew, crawling up its vast web and back into the cover of the mammoth trees. Rydel gained his feet and knew who it was immediately.

The green-armored Terma turned and took off her helmet, revealing a fall of scarlet hair. "Who's the stubborn fool, now?" Elisaria said with a satisfied grin.

Dropping his sticky, bloody dagger, he rushed forward and took her shoulders in both arms. "What are you doing here?" The deep darkness had retreated for now. Drymaus had warned him, he realized, responding to the nature of the threat by making a strange artificial night descend, but the golden glow was still muted. A shadow remained, like dark clouds clinging to the enchanted woods. Mist swirled about their feet, curling and growing ominously by the minute. "You shouldn't have come," he declared. "You need to go, now."

Elisaria's smile fell, looking confused and her confusion turned to anger. "Are you serious? That's the worst 'thank you for saving my life' I've ever heard."

"This is my challenge, Elisaria."

"A challenge you'd only be taking part in from the belly of a giant spider if it weren't for me."

Rydel growled. She was right, and yet... "Then I should have died," he snapped.

She gave a scoff. "Congratulations. That's officially the most idiotic thing you've ever said. Perhaps next time I will let you get your head snapped off."

Time was wasting, the darkness was returning. He realized what was done was done. They didn't have time for this. He needed to send her back and head deeper into the woods.

"You don't understand. More dangers will be coming. The books, the stories, they all say the same. There are dangers out there to make giant spiders seem tame. Leave, *now*." He knew his words were harsh, biting, but he would hurt her heart to keep her safe.

Instead, Elisaria's hurt expression turned to one of resoluteness. The mask of the fierce fighter, the second-in-command of the Terma was back in place. Flipping her sword in the air, she caught it by the handle in a reverse grip then smoothly slid it into its sheath. "Then we'll face them. Together. I know what you're doing, Rydel, and I appreciate it, but it won't work."

"Please," he said, gripping her hand, trying a softer tactic, "I can't promise I can protect you, and I can't lose you."

She shrugged. "Then don't promise. Like I told Cylar, while your gallantry is sweet, I can handle myself."

But Rydel wasn't so certain. Drymaus was different. Still, he knew that look in her eyes. There was no way she'd leave, not now. He debated doing something drastic, but dragging her out of the forest kicking and screaming would never work. Even if he could, he knew that Drymaus and its inhabitants could sense weakness. Ladened and distracted, he would attract nightmarish beasts like moths to a flame. It would never work.

She fixed him with her sky-blue eyes, seeing his worry. "As this is your choice, so this is mine. I am not going anywhere, not without you—so you might as well get used to it."

Rydel growled. Part of him was elated, and the rest of him was terrified. Somehow risking himself and risking her were two entirely different things. He couldn't bear to lose her, but she was right. For better or worse, she was with him now. With a deep breath, he shook his head and grabbed his fallen, crusted blade. "Come then, we can't stay here."

She fell in at his side, moving through the leaf litter and beneath the dark canopy with practiced ease and perfect silence. "Where are we headed?"

"To the heart of the woods. We must find the Hidden Pool and gather a vial of its contents," he said, extracting a small glass vial from his pocket.

Elisaria's radiant face lit up with awe. "It truly exists? The Well of Immortality?"

"Unless Master is lying, which he never is, then yes. It is very real."

They moved with haste, threading through the trees, many of which were crooked and bent like a witch's finger. Elisaria moved silently and swiftly as expected for one of her ranks, keeping pace with him at every step. About them, Drymaus seemed to thrum. An energy filled the air, neither good nor evil, but the dense spark of life suffused them with a vitality that quickened their gait. Rydel knew every second in these woods was a second that could spell their doom.

In a verdant clearing, butterflies the size of his head flitted through the glowing air. In the next, a large cat-like creature with downy fur but no claws pawed at the ground, digging and nibbling at honey-colored roots. They even passed the ever-rare and elusive sprytes—little glowing balls of pure energy that frolicked up and down trees or in patches of moss and rotting logs. They were leafsprytes, the color of grass. Elsewhere they saw puffs of blue, watersprytes, who bobbed in aquamarine streams, or over a perfectly still lake the shade of lavender in full bloom. They made music as they danced, filling the air with a melody impossible to repeat, but lulled the soul and sounded like mischief incarnate. Each time, Elisaria's eyes grew wide, as did his own. Yet as enchanting as it all was, every moment was a moment too long, a moment that made Rydel's skin itch. This in mind, he pulled her along faster, never lingering.

Rydel's keen tracking sense guided them deeper into the heart of the forest.

Elisaria grabbed his arm suddenly, dragging him to a halt. He knew not to question as they ducked behind a tree. There, his foot landed in foul bog-like muck that bubbled and frothed. Insects and other many-legged creatures crawled about the puddles' shore and he covered his nose from the stench. A moment later, out of the woods a giant creature made of twining twigs, vine and leaf emerged. A balrot. Friendly as balrots were, they waited impatiently until the creature passed. Stories said one thing, but the reality might tell another. Rydel almost moved, eager as he was to continue, but he smelled a danger, and Drymaus echoed his fear. A shadowy hue descended upon the woods. Elisaria sensed it as well as she stiffened, fingers digging into his arm. "Not yet," she whispered. "Something's coming."

The darkness grew. It had been sunny a moment before, but the woods now resembled a deepening night. Another moment later, stalking out of the trees came a nightmare. Its hide was the color of pale elven flesh in spots, and in others, it looked like dried moss. Scales spotted its body like a fish that had been rotting in the sun. As it moved, the thick, scaly hide rippled, blending with the woods as it stepped on long spindly legs—the hue vaguely mimicking the surroundings it passed. It had large pale eyes, cloudy and filmed as if it was sightless. The creature's human-shaped head held a wide mouth that rhythmically opened and closed, revealing needles instead of teeth covered in blood as if it had recently feasted. On its bare skull were long, sharp ears and a row of fleshy spines that continued down its hunched back. The spines continued down a long tail that undulated along the ground. It was easily twice Rydel's height and it moved on all fours. It looked like some strange misshapen spawn of an elf, demon, and dragon. Talons on the end of its spindly legs raked the earth, churning up moss and making the earth sizzle with every step. Rydel recognized it from the stories and pictures in his lore books. A drekkar. Rydel had been certain they were myth.

Stories said they were once elves who had tried to steal the magic and power of dragons. They had drank dragon blood and performed some dark ritual only for it to end horribly wrong—drekkar was the result. Beings neither elf nor dragon, nor of this world, and horribly twisted by the dark magic.

The nightmarish drekkar paused a dozen paces away. It sniffed the air with its holes where a nose should be as if sensing something. A moment later, its scaly skin rippled, melding with the woods and going nearly invisible. *Hunting form,* Rydel knew, panicked as its head swiveled their way and they ducked back behind the tree. Blood pounded in his ears. Rydel knew drekkar had an impeccable sense of smell, but stories said nothing about them being blind. Could it see? Cautiously, he glanced around the tree, peering through the foliage. His breath caught—the drekkar had taken several steps closer in their direction, sniffing as it stalked.

Smell...

It can smell our breath, smell us, he realized.

He grabbed muck from the oozing pit and rubbed it on himself, gesturing fervently for Elisaria to do the same. She did, smearing the smelly mud over her body, coating her green-plated armor and her face with the foul substance. Rydel suppressed a gag from the stench and as he looked to peer around the tree... The drekkar was there. It towered over him, and each footfall crushed the grass, burning it into ash as it stalked around the tree to face them. It opened its bloody maw with a hiss to reveal rows upon rows of razor-sharp teeth. Rydel held his breath and Elisaria did the same. If it truly was half-elf with its long, pointed ears, it would hear their breathing. The drekkar cocked its head, looming over them, sniffing, trying to catch their smell. Foggy white eyes stared without seeing. It crooned, a terrible clacking cry from deep within its throat. Its jaws snapped a breath away from Elisaria's face. Every muscle in Rydel's body wanted to cut the creature down, to tear it to pieces but knew they hunted in packs. If he cut this one down, more would come—many more. So he resisted every urge inside him. Elisaria's eyes were wide in terror and then she shut them, continuing to hold her breath. Soon the air in Rydel's lungs burned, and he wanted desperately to suck in a breath but he refrained. The drekkar flicked a long too-elven like a tongue. It tasted Elisaria and every muscle in her body was rigid. But the demonic creature only garnered a fleck of mud on its tongue. Immediately hissing, the drekkar recoiled, shaking its large head in disgust and then slowly stalked away. After another few painstaking moments of lungs burning for air, Rydel gasped and Elisaria did the same—gulping sweet, life-giving breaths. He grabbed her but she pulled away. "Are you..."

"Fine," she said, her voice rattled. "I'm fine. Let's keep going."

Rydel felt troubled, but he gave her an encouraging smile and they ran, deeper into the woods, faster and harder—sprinting until—

The trees stopped.

A vast glade opened and there... in the center of the glade was a pool surrounded by glowing rocks. From the pool itself issued a soft blush of blue, a cerulean hue. "That's it. The Hidden Pool."

"The Well of Immortality," Elisaria whispered in disbelief. She stepped forward and Rydel grabbed her arm. "What are you doing?" She asked. "Isn't this what we came for?"

"Nothing's ever this easy," he said.

"Easy?" She snorted. "You call that easy?"

"I didn't train all my life just for that," he replied. Then he sensed something. Something different from what he'd ever sensed. It wasn't like the drekkar or any of the other magical beings thus far. Beings that existed of spark—the essence of life. This was something else. The hairs on his arms stood on end and his skin pricked. The flow. It was the magic of the gods, of divine or primordial beings. Beings that existed since the beginning of time, since creation. There weren't many of those. Ronin were one force, darkwalkers and phoxes another... and... "We're not alone," Rydel announced, every muscle in his body tensing.

Dragons were the last.

Every instinct in him that had been trained assess danger, to fight or flee, told him to run and run *now*. But he knew there was no escaping this creature.

Behind the Hidden Pool sat a tree. It had many names. It wasEliwarian the Elder Tree. Other cultures and races had their names as well: Ig'mal, Fondorus and more than could be counted. To most, it was simply The World Tree. A behemoth that connected the world of the living to the world of the dead—its limbs touching the heavens, and roots the underworld beneath, binding the spiritual realms. Rydel tried to take in the trunk that was so wide it spanned much of the of the clearings width and beyond. If he was not an elf and prepared for such a sight, he would have thought it a wall of wood for the way it stretched beyond sight. The tree had birthed the world—a god in its own right.

Animals existed here. Several stags bounded through the woods, a large owl perched on the bough above watching inquisitively, and two squirrels chittered at one another. As the darkness swelled and shadows and light joined, Drymaus was announcing the arrival of something else.

The squirrels scrambled into their burrows, the stags bounded off, and the owl took flight. Elisaria watched with him, her breath quickening. "You need to leave," Rydel demanded. He turned to her. "Please, Elisaria. I beg of you."

"I'm not going anywhere," she answered, stepping closer to him, but he heard a note of fear in her voice.

Just then, out of the immense otherworldly tree came a thundering boom. And another. Footsteps. Immense, terrible, earth-rattling footsteps.

"What is it?" Elisaria asked, stepping back with him, her voice shaken.

"A creature bound to the wheel of time."

Out of the shadow of the tree's recesses stepped a giant claw the size of a building, and a scaled body followed it shortly after. Rydel's eyes tracked the creature all the way to its massive head that towered stories above them.

A dragon.

The creature was perfectly white, with scales that shone like the sun hitting the first snow. The alabaster plates were each the size of Rydel's head, interlocking and overlapping in a seamless display that would shame and awe the master smiths of Eldas to tears. As it moved, the scales and its body flowed, curling around the Hidden Pool protectively. At last, the dragon fixed them with its huge cloudy-white eyes, gazing down upon the mortals. Rydel felt drawn by those white eyes, sucked in as if falling into fathomless depths of knowledge and time. At his feet, he was distantly aware of the eddies of wind swirling, tossing leaves into the air. "Welcome, mortals," the creature intoned. The sound of its voice was bone-rattling. It trembled the woods and made leaves quake and fall from nearby trees. But most miraculous of all, it sounded both within Rydel's head and without. "What is it you wish?"

Rydel stepped forward, letting go of Elisaria's hand. "I've come for the Hidden Pool."

"It lies before you, what are you waiting for?" The boom of its voice held a hint of mirth and a mischievous glint flickered in the dragon's eye.

Rydel desperately wanted to trust the creature but hesitated.

"Don't," Elisaria said. "It's a trap."

Kneeling in the dirt, Rydel bowed his head and stuck his blade into the rich soil. "With your permission only, great dragon. I humbly request a vial of its contents, nothing more, nothing less. Grant us this, Lord of the Woods, and we will leave the way we came."

"Elves, the most cautious of all races. And Lord of the Woods, is it? What a small realm you give me providence over. I am of all lands, of all things, as are you. I am air and wind itself. As for the way you came—it is gone."

Rydel gulped but he held his ground. "What must I do?"

"Defeat me," the creature boomed in a voice that was both in his head and aloud, making his teeth shudder.

Rydel felt his blood freeze at the reply. "Surely there's another way."

"Another way?" The dragon's body shook and he realized it was... laughing. "Come now, little elf, you didn't think taking a sip of immortality would be free, did you? All things have their cost. This water is our life-blood, the lifeblood of Farhaven. I will grant you your vial, your precious sip if you defeat me or one of my brothers."

Rydel's hope and despair were balanced on a knife's edge, fists clenching at his side in rising fury. Nothing about this was right. Defeat a primordial creature? It was impossible. Not to mention, dragons held neither good nor evil. Unlike the drekkar, he had no ill will towards such a being. If anything, he was in awe. While it was as likely to snap him in two as leave him be, Rydel couldn't imagine vanquishing a creature that had existed since the beginning of time. Dragons were said to be bound to Farhaven's fate—their lives tied to the survival of the world itself. Defeating this beast would be, in essence, striking a blow to Farhaven itself. "I won't fight you," Rydel said adamantly.

"Then, little elf, you will leave this place as you found it and never return."

"No," he said fiercely stepping forward, "I cannot leave without the vial."

"It seems you are in a predicament, little elf. Choose wisely and choose now."

Rydel turned to Elisaria. "You've done everything you can," she said. "There's nothing more to do." She pulled his arm, eyes crinkling with a worried smile. "Come, we can tell this story to our children one day and no one will ever believe us." Her pull took him a step away and he nodded, when... words echoed in his mind... a memory from long ago returned.

Master Trinaden sitting before the fire.

"Rydel," Trinaden spoke. Then he was silent for a long time, staring at the flames until finally, "Your lives are no longer your lives. If you survive this, you'll be able to change the course of history. Dryan needs to know that this isn't about you. It isn't about me. If you survive, you may likely save us all."

Rydel stopped Elisaria's pull. Immediately, he saw her face break into such sorrow that it threatened to break his heart once more. She knew what he would say. "I've got one last thing to do."

"Rydel... please, don't do this. You will die!"

And he found a smile, cupping her cheek. "Everything I am, everything I've trained for—my whole life—has come down to this moment. If you care for me, know that who you care for is the elf that needs to do this."

Elsaria's face warred with pain, sorrow, and hope. Finally, she nodded, but as he stepped away, she sobbed.

Rydel faced the great beast and took a deep breath. "I'm ready."

"Come then, little elf. Show me the power of the Hidden who trained you."

————

Rydel had been trained for every possible scenario by the best warrior the world had ever known, but fighting a dragon was something else entirely. Still, he had a blade. He had scrapped off the spider's encrusted webbing and now its edge was as sharp as ever, gleaming like a second-sun, made by master elf craftsman—the best blacksmiths in Farhaven. If he could find an opening, the blade would cut. He prayed.

Rydel charged, and the dragon rose onto its hind legs, issuing a bout of flames from its wide maw. Expecting this, Rydel lunged and dove away from the scorching flames in the nick of time feeling their heat on his back. He rose smoothly as more flames issued forth. Again and again, he dove, moving with lightning speed, faster still. His muscles reached their breaking point. As a new bout issued forth, he dug his feet in and cut a deep arcing slice into the ground creating a fan of sod that doused the flames. Through this he dove, entering the dragon's range. He cut with all his might letting loose a terrible cry. As the blade made contact with the thick opal-like scales, sparks issued, but his slice harmlessly slid across the creature. Surprise and disappointment spiraled through him, but he didn't waste a moment. Clawed talons like pillars came crashing down where he stood and he rolled to the left, barely evading their rumbling blow. He saw the damage they caused—rivets into the ground that would have buried a full-grown elf, followed by ragged furrows that broke the nearest stone guarding the Hidden Pool. Each claw gleamed with such an edge that it put his blade to shame. An idea struck, and immediately he was back on his feet and running up the clawed hand, up the scaly arm.

The dragon's other claws raked towards him and he leapt—air rushed past him as he fell a dozen feet then—snatched onto its wide white wings, the sockets of his arms threatening to pop, but he held on and cut. The tough leathery wings resisted his cut at first, but finally, the sword's edge found purchase and the blade bit. He fell as if slicing through the cloth of a ship's sail, slowing his descent as he cut. The dragon roared and whipped its wing. Snapped violently by the motion, Rydel catapulted through the air, landing hard on the ground. Rolling absorbed some of the brutal impact, but he felt something snap in his chest and knew he'd broken a rib or two. The world blurred but Elisaria's cry brought him back. With painful breaths, he grabbed his fallen blade and staggered to his feet.

The dragon turned, but Rydel was now at its back. Its scaled back looked like a spiraling ramp, curling up its long tail towards its head. Pain lancing through his chest, Rydel sprinted as the beast moved. With Elvin agility he raced up its spine, slaloming through the row of knee-high white spines that lined the creature's back. The dragon flailed as he ran, tail and body whipping back and forth to throw him free, but Rydel didn't slow, balancing with difficulty. Reaching the top, claws tried to scratch the dragon's back where he ran, raking at him. Rydel leapt their strike, diving aside and dangling by a long spike—and the creature's own claws slashed its scaled body. Razor sharp as they were, the talons clanged off harmlessly, ruining his plan. Gritting his teeth and crying out, Rydel pulled himself up from where he dangled, ran the last of the beast's spine and reached its head.

Wind rushed about him as the dragon whipped its head. Rydel grabbed a long white spike, holding on, muscles straining and looked down. Here the scales were smaller, finer, and thinner. The beast's momentum switched direction, and it gave him a precious moment, a single breath, to strike. Hoping to his very soul, Rydel released the white spike in that sliver of breath and raised his blade. Then, with the gleaming elven sword, he struck—with every ounce of his strength towards the dome of the creature's skull. Hoping to plunge his blade into the dragon's brain. The blade fell with terrible speed and then—

Rydel was falling. The dragon had vanished beneath him as if turned into thin air. Rydel hit the ground hard enough to send every bone in his body shuddering and rattling, and his head thundered with pain. When he looked up, he saw the dragon reappear at the end of the massive clearing in a gust of wind. The wind materialized, forming scales, large white wings, and a massive head with rows of teeth—and those eyes. Those fathomless, white, swirling eyes, watched him knowingly.

A dragon of wind...

One of the nine, and leader of the nine. Rydel should have known.

"Valiant," the dragon said in a deep rumble and lifted its wings.

Rydel rose to his feet and spotted the tear on its left wing where he had cut it. A flicker of pride filled him. He could cut it. Perhaps if... As he watched though, the jagged and violent wound suddenly knit together with little bits of wind surrounding it, until the dragon's wing was whole once more. Everything he had done was undone in a split second. Meanwhile, his body felt as if he'd thrown it down a cliffside and hit every rock on the way to the bottom. He was bruised and battered. Breathing deeply sent splinters of pain through his whole body. Elisaria had her hands clasped over her mouth, watching in fear. Rydel knew to his core there was no way he could defeat this thing. Moreover, he saw the look in the dragon's eyes—it had no intention of sparing his life. The bargain had been struck and now the creature would follow through.

"You are truly something, little elf," the dragon rumbled. "Perhaps you should have chosen my brothers or sisters as challengers, but against me, you have no chance." The taunt reminded Rydel of Aladar and Hadrian's first clash so long ago. Save this time, the dragon was toying with *him*, not the other way around. The deep booming voice held a note of sorrow, "I will regret your death, little elf, but our deal was struck and I am of my oath. We dragons are of our words, our code, or we are nothing. Our oaths bind us to the land, and the land to us."

We are more than our codes... Elisaria's words. Then came Master Trinaden's voice, echoing in his head, *it may break you all if you do not find the final code.* The final code. That was it... What was the final code? The third code of the Hidden. Clues had been laid before him, but now he needed to decipher them.

The first code: *strength is life, weakness death.*

The second code: *fight only when necessary.*

Each was meant to balance the other, and the final to bring the two to perfect harmony. Then what was it!? He needed to know. The dragon's monstrous maw opened, showing what looked like a grin.

Then disappearing into a gust of air, the dragon of wind reappeared over him like a mountain. Claws raked, digging into the ground, as it crossed the final span. The dragon opened its terrible jaws showing teeth like sharpened javelins ready to skewer him. As the beast's maw closed Trinaden's words returned, *you saved your brother despite the pain you knew it would cause you. But you can't lose your soul just to save the world, or the world isn't worth saving.* The dragon wanted him to step forward and take the water, but Rydel wanted to prove his worth. Pride and ego warred inside him. Again, even being here with Elisaria, he wanted to fight, to lose himself at all costs. But was that right? Master had taught him that strength and sacrifice weren't enough. He needed to have a good heart. To have a good soul.

Yet he couldn't give up. This creature wouldn't stop until he was dead, nor could he stop until it was dead.

Bellowing, Rydel dove out of the way of the snapping jaws, but not to the side or backwards. Instead, he dove forward, beneath the creature. White scales soared over him. The dragon of wind then rose ... then he saw it. A scale seemed to shimmer, and... vanish? There! A chink in the armor— there was a missing scale of wind showing a pulsing red flesh of the beast. The red flesh had an orange glow to it as if made of pure spark or flow. Of magic. But the flesh beneath that orange glow seemed real enough, and precisely where a creature's heart should lie.

Rydel knew the unexpected *reckless* roll towards the dragon had stunned it, and it was looking for him. Above him the creature bellowed, twisting its head as if searching for Rydel. How long did he have until it realized he was beneath? The flesh was close, the massive heart of the creature thumping with vitality like a giant war drum. He could leap for it, but it was too far. Rydel's breathing slowed, biding his time, watching the heart. Yet at any moment he knew the creature would discover his location and smash him into the earth, or snap him in half with its jaws and dagger-like teeth. Then it struck him... He could throw the blade. Rydel gripped the haft, gaze riveted to the thumping heart that hovered above him. Muscles in his arms, shoulders, and back coiled, ready to launch the blade with every ounce of strength he had. He'd done it before. He knew if he threw it true, it would the pierce the heart and slay the creature; allowing him to obtain the water from the Hidden Pool. Every fiber in him begged to launch the sword in his white-knuckled grip, to take his fading chance. Any moment now it would turn and notice him.

And yet...

To lay low the magnificent legendary beast. How could he? A primordial creature. A living being born at the beginning of creation that was bound to Farhaven. How was he supposed to save Farhaven by killing one of its favored creations? By, in essence, cutting a piece out of Farhaven's own heart? And yet, if he didn't, he would fail.

Rydel knew his opening would vanish any second. Hating himself, he prepared to throw the blade and end it. Above him, the dragon roared and swiveled its massive body like a snake as if searching. Why hadn't dragon disappeared into a gust of wind? Why hadn't it found him or thrashed up the ground in a flurry?

As if... searching. The words, his own thoughts struck him.

A memory returned of his Master and him in the small hut that day after he saved Dryan.

Trinaden's next words were a mere whisper, *"The third and final code."* And his eyes blazed with the fire's light, *"To be a Hidden, above all else means to sacrifice yourself, but never your soul for the greater good."*

The greater good.

Killing this beast wasn't the greater good. It couldn't be.

Staring at the thumping, exposed heart, Rydel let the sword tumble from his grip and bellowed, *"Sacrifice yourself, but never your soul."*

At his words, wind erupted in a violent rush, making his cloak flap widely, stinging his eyes with its gale-like force. When Rydel opened his eyes, he saw the dragon was before him. Rydel gawked, eyes panning up. The dragon... It was more massive than ever before. Rydel realized the creature had scaled itself *down* for their fight. The maw seemed to curve into a terrifying smile and Rydel saw the missing scale. As he stared, wind swirled and it reappeared and the beast was whole once more. As he thought, the creature had intentionally left itself vulnerable, testing him. The dragon of wind rumbled, "The final code. Very good. I suppose I could have gone easier on you, yet I sensed you were the strongest, so a harder trial seemed the right thing to do." Rydel bowed his head. "Take your vial," it rumbled.

Rydel moved forward, towards the glowing pool at the base of the Elder Tree.

"Not there," said the beast, mirth lacing its rattling voice. Just then, there was a swirl of wind before Rydel's feet and a murky, muddy pool appeared. In its depths, there was a glimmer of light.

Rydel understood with a small laugh. "That pool," he said, nodding to the glamorous turquoise waters at the base of the Elder Tree. "That was a trick the whole time, wasn't it? Even if I defeated you, I would never have succeeded, would I?"

"Perception is a tricky thing," the dragon of wind uttered.

Rydel reeled at those words... they were his words to Elisaria when Hadrian had been fighting the commander of the Terma. "How..." He whispered, then swallowing his awe, Rydel obeyed and pulling the glass bottle from his pocket he neared the waters and filled the small vial. "Thank you," Rydel uttered.

The giant beast bowed its head. Then abruptly, the dragon of wind vanished in a burst of wind and white eddies. As it vanished, so too did the murky pool before him.

Rydel sagged to his knees, exhausted.

"Are you all right?" Elisaria asked, her hands worriedly searching him for wounds. When she found none but cuts and scrapes, she embraced him tightly. Rydel grunted in pain from the shattered rib and Elisaria apologized profusely, pulling away. "Dear spirits, you moved like the wind... You... you just fought a dragon, my love."

"And lost," he said with a smirk. "It was toying with me the whole time."

"I don't think there was any winning against that. Not in the traditional sense."

Rydel grunted his agreement. "Perhaps you're right. The only thing I have defeated, was... well, nothing. You've defeated the spider and you were the one that heard the drekkar's approach."

"Sounds about right," she said. "Perhaps I'm a Hidden now too."

Grinning, he kissed her. "Let's go home."

"Please and thank you." Then Elisaria paused, grabbing him. "Wait a moment. You're a mess, what are we doing?" She filched the full bottle from his hand.

"What are you doing?" He asked anxiously.

"We can't have you limping out of this place, can we? I'm all for saving your hide, but if you get hurt, you're too heavy for me to carry out of here. Besides, you don't need the whole vial, do you? Just a drop or two should suffice, I imagine." She put the vial to his lips and immediately he felt a warm sensation infuse him. Something not like pain, but not like pleasure, tugged at his wounds, pricking and growing until... He felt his ribs and expected to wince.

"Nothing," he said. "They're healed."

"It is a miracle. See, you have to trust me more," she said and waggled the bottle.

He felt invigorated too.

They walked for a while, leaving the glade behind them and teasing one another when suddenly the woods darkened. Rydel's heart began to beat faster, and it wasn't the enchanted water's doing. From out of the shadow of the trees stalked a tall, menacing familiar evil on all fours. A drekkar. Elisaria hadn't seen it yet, facing him, but she saw his eyes taper to dangerous slits. "Rydel?"

Rydel unsheathed his blade. "Get behind me."

Elisaria whirled about, seeing the advancing threat. Instead of listening to him, however, she pulled her own blade free. "We can take one." As she said it, another drekkar crept out of the umbra of night, and then another. Long skeletal fingers tipped with black claws raked the ground, and where they did the once green grass sizzled to a charcoaled black. The first drekkar's head tilted and Rydel felt its pale, sightless gaze fixed on them. Slavering jaws dripped with a wanton lust. "Three we can take still, but how do they sense us?" Elisaria whispered.

Rydel might have been healed, but he'd been bleeding profusely from the dragon's attacks. "The blood," he whispered. "They smell the blood. And they're not just three. Drekkar hunt in packs."

As if summoned, more of the demons stalked out of the woods joining their brothers. At his side, he felt Elisaria's tension but she only gripped the haft of her blade tighter.

"We'll have to clear a path," he said and Elisaria nodded. "Don't get touched, whatever you do." Heart pounding, Rydel charged and laid into them with abandon. The demons were fast and their reach was long, but Rydel was hungry for their blood. Dipping beneath the first creature's strike, he lopped its head off and dodged the spray of dark blood. The next he ran through with his blade before it could strike. Sensing claws behind him, Rydel stabbed behind without looking, feeling flesh puncture. But drekkar were tenacious and both creatures slashed at him, snarling. Rydel pulled his blade free, severed their boney claws with quick slashes and left the two demons to bleed as he leapt to the next. Elisaria was handling her own, battling two when—

Out of the corner of his vision, Rydel saw one of the creature's he'd left to bleed pull itself on bloody stumps towards Elisaria, sniffing with the empty holes in its face, smelling her nearness. Elisaria deftly fended the two beasts before her but didn't see the threat behind. Rydel cried out but she was distracted as the beast rose on bloody stumps and snapped, biting into her leg. The needle-like teeth pierced the armor. Elisaria shrieked but didn't hesitate to turn and stab the demon through the head, ending its miserable life. The bite, however, was enough to distract her. Rydel was almost to her when one of the drekkar she'd been fighting hungrily saw its opening and slashed.

Elisaria turned, but she was too slow. She cried out, the sound piercing Rydel's soul as a claw raked across her stomach.

No...

Elisaria fell, gasping and clutching her abdomen. His heart froze, every muscle in his body exploded into action. He was almost to her. At the same time, more drekkar fell upon him from all sides. He couldn't do anything, he wanted to grab her and flee, but they were surrounded, overwhelmed. The end seemed near. *No... I am more than this,* he thought. *I won't let it end this way.*

Roaring, Rydel lost himself to his unbridled rage. They fell upon him in droves, but Rydel welcomed it and cried for their blood. Sword a blur, he sliced, stabbed, and evaded, his body a whirling dervish of death. Heads, arms, tough leather hide and patchy scales, all of it were like soft fruit beneath his blade as he sliced his way to Elisaria's side. Yet more came, and while the blood from her wound oozed, screeching drekkar fell upon the glade.

Something came over him, something he'd never felt. He became something more—something not elf. Once, he'd seen his master move this fast. Now he moved faster. Fatigued muscles burned like acid with each strike until the sword felt like a sledgehammer. Still, he shoved the fatigue down and lost himself to the dance of death. Rydel's blade moved of its own accord. Every moment, every second of those brutal lessons that had been hammered into him now became thoughtless. Instinctual even. It had made him a weapon. It had made him death.

Black blood and red rage filled his vision, barely dipping strikes that grazed his throat, head, or leg. The slosh of blood, the dull cutting of flesh became the only music to his ears. Their cries that had once sounded hungry now held a note of terror. Drekkar began to slow their advance, suddenly hesitant to near the maelstrom of steel. So he advanced on them. Foul blood splashed and struck his body. Dark and syrupy, it seared with its touch, burning at his clothes, so he ripped the tattered remnants of a vest free. Still, he struck. Only when the last drekkar fell, a slice opening its belly and emptying vile blood and guts to the already blood-soaked ground, did he drop his blade. Rydel collapsed at Elisaria's side. Every muscle burned, and his voice was ragged. Only then did he realize he'd been screaming while he killed.

She smiled weakly at his approach. "It seems I'm not a Hidden after all..." Her words were soft, pained.

"Don't speak," he answered, "please." His own voice was hoarse and choked. Swiftly he felt her skin. It was cold and growing colder. Where the drekkar had cut, her terma armor was opened. Each interlocking plate that could deter the sharpest blade was now peeled back to look like twisted scrap metal. Drekkar's magical touch had made her armor look like parchment. The wound was long and ugly, yet it didn't bleed. The edges of it were black, necrotic, and the dark rot was spreading. Rydel grits his jaw and stuffed down his terror and sorrow, controlling his emotions.

She cupped his cheek, pulling his gaze back to her and smiled. "This is not your fault."

The words were like a dagger. Rydel smirked. "You're going to be all right. I've suffered worse under Master's training."

"You might be the world's worst liar, my love. I..." she coughed and dark blood came forth, spitting it onto her pale skin.

"No," he breathed, then he remembered—the realization hitting him like a lightning bolt.

The vial.

72

Panicked, Rydel frantically scoured the ground until—

There.

Falling over himself, he snatched the glass container from the ground only to see that the vial had been spilled in the fight. His heart seized in his chest. It was empty. Still, he put it to her mouth, trying to drain something, anything into her parted lips, but it had all been drained onto the bloody ground. It was gone. She gripped his hand, stopping him. "No more," she said, "I was the one who spilled it. I know it's empty."

"Then I'll get more." He began to rise.

"No!" Her weak voice begged. "It's too far. I'll be gone before you do. Please, stay here... stay with me. I... I don't want to be alone when it comes..."

Rydel shook his head, feeling hot tears fall onto her perfect face and smooth skin. "I can't... I can't lose you."

Elisaria smiled softly. "For all your strength, you can't control this, my love. The Great Spirit calls, and I must answer."

"What am I supposed to do without you?"

"Live," she said. "You... you are something special. Something this world has never seen. You will change it for the better. I know you will. Just live, for me," she said and her breathing grew tight. Her hand squeezed his more tightly as pain flashed across her faultless features. "Promise me." Rydel did, promising fervently. Then her eyes took on a shadow as if seeing something. Her voice quavered suddenly, "I-I'm afraid, my love. H-hold me?"

Rydel did, pulling her tight and feeling hot tears fall down onto her.

Then he felt her chest stop rising and falling. Rydel swiftly pulled away and saw Elisaria's eyes gazing into the world of the beyond, seeing the Great Spirit. She was gone.

"No, no, no, no," he uttered suddenly frantic. "I'm not done yet," he said through grit teeth and gently picking her up, he ran. *I have to find the pools.* Then he would submerge her body and give Elisaria her fill of the life-giving waters.

73

When he returned to where he fought the dragon of wind in the vast enclave, however, the Hidden Pool was gone. No sign of the dragon's battle even showed. Had he imagined it? "No, it was here!" He cursed. "Gods, it was here, I swear it."

But somehow he knew. Like a Node, a magical sanctuary of Farhaven, the Hidden Pool must only appear based on need. Well, he needed it now—he needed it like he needed air. Rydel bellowed into the woods until his already hoarse voice cracked and vanished, but there was no answer. He fell to his knees, Elisaria's limp body in his arms.

In a daze, the world empty of color and life, Rydel staggered back out of the woods. This time nothing attacked. Drekkar watched with their sightless pale eyes, drawn by the blood. They only watched, sniffing the air. Black, foul blood still coated his body. It had left little burns that would turn to scars. The burns had exposed his muscles that still coiled and bunched with rage. Clicking sounds tracked him, hungry and horrible, but they drew no closer. In a daze, he walked until he saw the light of the forest's edge.

At last, he broke the tree line and collapsed to his knees again in the center of the empty clearing. Only hours ago he had left his brothers and his master here, to travel into the woods. Now it felt like a lifetime.

Rydel laid Elisaria down on the cool grass. She was pale in the morning sun. Her skin looked like the first snow, but her eyes... Her stunning sky-blue eyes now stared up, past the morning sky, gazing at nothing. Those eyes, robbed of all her previous fire. She was dead, with nothing he could do to bring her back, and as he'd never done before, Rydel began to sob. Heaving sobs that retched his whole body as he clutched at her, feeling more helpless than he'd ever felt.

Time passed, the night settled on him, dawn came next—a new day—and still he held her in his arms.

For Rydel, the world, his world, had ended.

Finally, after an eternity, he opened his eyes. Dawn and snow settled about him. A single snowflake fell from the sky, touching and melting on his cheek. White pallets of powder coated everything; the skeletal trees, the

74

clearing, even himself. How long had he been there? How many days had he gone without eating or drinking? Shirtless as he was, he should have frozen to death long ago, but he felt only a numb cold. On his pale skin, he noticed countless white lines of varying size, but they all had the same look. And he realized it was the wounds, now healed from where the blood of the drekkar had touched. The little scars marred his hard flesh and muscle. He was glad for them, representing a memory he didn't want to banish, and a far too small a price for the agony inside him. But why wasn't he dead of frostbite? Then he glanced to the darkened Drymaus Forest. The woods had a powerful magic... It had saved him, but why?

Above the clear sky showed a new day. Rydel looked down at Elsaria. He wasn't sure how long it had been, but the same powerful magic of the nearby woods had kept her body the same as the day she had died, just as pale and lifeless, but just as beautiful. Rydel's muscles hurt, tendons and ligaments searing with pain as he slowly stretched. Every moment was agony as he took what felt like his first real breath in ages.

Then... as he turned he saw something on a skeletal tree in the center of the glade.

A cloak dangled from the tree's frail branch. A familiar cloak.

A hando cloak.

And on the stump before it, coated in snow, rested a blade in a sheath. A leafblade. Master Trinaden. The elf had come and gone silently. *Like a knife in the dark.* Perhaps he'd seen Rydel's pain and didn't want to disturb him. The thought was a distant comfort to Rydel's cold heart—knowing Trinaden had seen Elisaria and would carry the news back to the Terma and her family.

Rydel turned from the articles and went back to Elisaria's body. Her corpse. He spent that night gathering twigs and branches of the proper size. Then he burned her body. Watching the flames flick at the snowy sky, he felt his heart break even further. The cold had no effect that his soul didn't already feel. He watched for a long time. As he did, he had the image of Master Trinaden's face that night and the single tear. He thought he understood. Finally, the flames died, and dawn came again. Then, out of the ashes, he spotted something. A glint of white. A stone. *His* stone. She'd held onto it. The paint was mostly burnt off and smeared, but a little had remained. Pulling it from the ash, he felt it between his thumb and forefinger. Then he pocketed the stone.

Elisaria dead, his mother without his message, no one knew he was alive. What was he to do now? The raging fire inside him—the thing that gave him purpose and drove him relentlessly forward—was cold now, like a great hearth frozen over.

Then he looked to the woods.

Empty and alone, he moved to the bare tree and retrieved the cloak that was laden with snow. Shaking it free, he threw the grand cloak about his shoulder, covering his naked torso. As he did, the woods blended around him. Then he strapped and buckled the leafblade to his waist. The sword, the very object he had coveted all his life, now seemed only a trinket.

Rydel laid the empty vial on the nearby ground and he remembered his master's words: 'the codes are all that matters.' That was it. The vial had just been an excuse, a test for the true reward. The true prize and test had been the final code, and now it was a part of him.

Sacrifice yourself, but never your soul—the code, the words thrummed through him.

Rydel eyed the woods. His brothers had to have passed the test.

They were out there still... That was why the Hidden Pool had abandoned him. And he remembered a declaration he had made a long time ago to two teary-eyed boys, "*He was wrong. This is our home. We are brothers now and we will protect each other. I won't let anything happen to you two.*" Hadrian smiled and Dryan nodded. "*I promise.*"

Dryan's words still stung.

"*You think you're better than me, and perhaps you are for now. But I will be stronger. One day, I will make you both tremble before me.*"

Worse, he knew his younger brother was right. Rydel had thought he was better deep down. That didn't matter though. None of it mattered. Dryan was his brother, heart and soul, forged by a bond thicker than blood. They had to be alive and he would find them.

All his life he'd had visions of this moment... The sword at his waist and cloak on his back—but he'd trade it all to have her again. At the least, he could vanquish the demons that did this. Vengeance wasn't right, and it wouldn't bring her back, but it was something. *Live,* she had said. He would, at least to save his brothers, to not let Dryan fall to darkness, and purge the woods of demons or anything that stood in his way.

Then Rydel turned and walked away, into the woods.

A   Hidden.

THE END

www.matt-wolf.com

Made in the USA
Columbia, SC
07 August 2020